Father's Best Friends Baby

An Enemies to Lovers, Age Gap Romance

Dakota Nash

Copyright © 2024 by Dakota Nash

All rights reserved.

No portion of this book may be reproduced in any form without written permission from the publisher or author, except as permitted by U.S. copyright law.

Contents

1.	Christos	1
2.	Pamela	8
3.	Pamela	16
4.	Christos	25
5.	Pamela	32
6.	Christos	39
7.	Pamela	44
8.	Christos	50
9.	Pamela	56
10.	Christos	62
11.	Pamela	68
12.	Pamela	75
13.	Christos	80
14.	Pamela	85
15.	Christos	91
16.	Pamela	96
17.	Christos	101
18.	Pamela	106

19.	Pamela	112
20.	Christos	116
21.	Pamela	121
22.	Christos	127
23.	Pamela	132
24.	Christos	137
25.	Pamela	143
26.	Christos	148
27.	Pamela	153
28.	Pamela	158
29.	Christos	163
30.	Pamela	168
SNEAK PEEK		175

Chapter 1
Christos

"Hollering at me from your third-floor window wasn't enough excitement for you for one day?" the woman on the beach demands. "You had to come down here and track me down? And why are you staring at me like that?"

I falter momentarily, unsure if I can continue with what I came here to do. I know it's her—I knew the moment I saw her standing on the beach. I'd recognize that red hair anywhere. It's like a golden flame on her head—vibrant copper color with glints of gold, and wild curls blowing in the wind. I've always had a thing for redheads, so it wasn't as if when I ran out here after her, I didn't know I would find her pretty. I did. But she's not just pretty, she's drop-dead gorgeous.

I wasn't expecting to be knocked sideways by my attraction to her. She's objectively a hottie, with full breasts that look like they'd fit perfectly in my hands. And oh my god, those tantalizing hips. Her lush lips already have me thinking about kissing her, and that is not what I came out here intending to do.

I mean, she's young. I recognized that about her even looking down from my third floor study. She's probably in her late twenties, a good fifteen to twenty years younger than I am. And I wouldn't usually look twice at a woman that much younger than me. I'm not the type of guy to have my eyes on people half my age.

Usually.

I don't know what it is about her. Maybe it's that she's looking at me like she's ready for a fight. That is so hot. I swear I came out here thinking I would intimidate her into telling me what the hell she was doing in Rose Crawford's house. I thought she would be so freaked out by the fact that I took the trouble to find her that she would immediately go belly-up and answer all my questions.

I don't think that now. She doesn't look remotely intimidated. She looks a little pissed off actually.

But it can't only be the fact that she's glaring daggers at me that makes me want to find a wall to pin her up against. People have given me dirty looks plenty of times in my life, and it's never provoked a reaction like this.

"And again, *why* are you staring at me?" she interrupts my fantasy.

That makes me pull it together because I *have* been staring, which is pretty embarrassing. I clear my throat. "I came looking for you because I thought we should have a real conversation," I tell her in a more conversational tone. "Unless you prefer being shouted at from windows, but it sounds like you weren't into that."

"Who in the world would be into that?" she asks, crossing her arms. "And what is it you need to talk to me about? We don't know each other, and I don't get the feeling you're here because you want to make friends."

"I think we got off to a bad start. Can we start over?" I may be only saying that because of how incredibly hot she is, and I judge myself for it, but I'm only a man.

She sighs. "I'm nowhere near the property, I'm nearly halfway around the peninsula," she says. "How long have you been following me?"

"I haven't been *following* you. I came looking for you."

"How did you find me?"

"You weren't hard to find," I tell her, pointing at her footprints in the sand. "You're the only person on this beach."

"There's *one* person on the beach, and you're so disturbed by that that you had to come out of your house and run me down?" She laughs half-heartedly. "What is it you think I'm doing, exactly, that you find so troubling?"

"What are you doing in the house next to mine?" It comes out sounding a little more aggressive than I mean it to. I want the answer, but it's not like I'm trying to accuse her of trespassing.

She folds her arms across her chest. "Renting it," she says. "Is that going to be a problem?"

Internally, I breathe a sigh of relief. Okay. She's only renting. She doesn't own the place. I can't imagine that Rose would have sold to someone other than me. She's perfectly aware that I have my eye on that house. It's the only piece of property along the coastline next to the National Seashore Park that I don't own. It feels like it should be mine by rights. Rose is not open to selling, but I'm sure that if she ever changed her mind, she would come to me first. I mean, she's got to. That's why I was so shocked to see someone else on that property. She *couldn't* have sold to someone else.

But she hasn't. She's only renting. I still don't love it, but at least it means the house will be available for me to buy when the time comes. That ship hasn't sailed.

"It's not going to be a problem," I tell her.

"So then, what are you doing out here?" she asks me. "Did you come out to tell me that my living in my own house wasn't a problem for you?"

"Are you always this aggressive?" Oh god, that is so hot. I want to lay her down right here, right now, and fuck her all day.

"Only when strange men come up to me on the beach and start questioning me about where I live."

I have to laugh at that. She's a character, but she does have a point about this. "Okay," I say. "Touché. I probably shouldn't have come up and bothered you."

She tucks her hands into the pockets of her jean shorts, an action that naturally draws my gaze downward. Damn, she's hot. Her legs seem to go on for miles beyond the cuffs of those shorts. Her shirt is cropped, exposing a tantalizing sliver of her belly between it and the waistline of her pants. I want to grab her and run my thumb along that line. I want to see if I can make her shiver.

And I need to get those thoughts out of my head pronto. Walking up to a young woman I don't know on the beach is bad enough, but standing here fantasizing about getting her naked is downright sketchy. And the two of us are going to be neighbors, whether either of us likes it or not, so it's to our benefit to figure out how to be around each other.

"It's all right," she says. "You caught me off guard, that's all. But it's okay."

"So...*can* we start over?"

"We can."

I hold out a hand to her. "I'm Christos," I say. "Christos Tzavaras."

"Pamela MacLaine," she says returning the handshake. "You can call me Pam."

"Hang on," I say, dropping her hand. "MacLaine?"

"Yes." She says knowingly. "I'm guessing you're familiar with my family's vineyard."

Oh, I'm more than familiar with it. "I know your father," I tell her. "Matt MacLaine, right? And I know your brother, Brian, too."

"Oh? They didn't mention that I'd be living next door to someone they knew."

"They didn't tell me you were coming home either," I tell her. "You're the one who was off in Padua, right?"

"You make it sound like I was on some type of vacation. I attended the University of Padova," she says.

"No, I knew that. Matt bragged about you all the time. Said you were learning all the latest skills and tricks to take the family business to the next level."

"How come you know so much about my father's business?"

"I volunteer at his vineyard."

Her eyebrows shoot up. "You do?"

I shrug. "I love wine," I explain. "I'm passionate about it, and your dad always says he needs as many hands as he can get. I get the feeling he's been especially hard-pressed since you've been away—not that he complains, of course, but having more people to help is always a benefit, right?"

"I didn't realize Dad had volunteers helping him," she says. "I knew he had a paid staff and seasonal employees, but I thought that was as far as it went."

"I don't think anyone else working there is a volunteer," I say. "And he's doing me a favor every bit as much as I'm doing him one, so it all shakes out in the balance."

She nods slowly. "Well, if we're neighbors and you're volunteering at the vineyard, I guess you and I are going to be seeing a fair bit of each other."

"Yeah, it's not feeling so reckless now that I came out to meet you." I grin. The truth is, I'm thrilled to have met her, and knowing that our paths are going to keep crossing is only serving to get me more excited about having her in my life. I still don't love the fact that she's living in the house I've been trying to buy for months, but since it's only a rental situation, I can make my peace with it. Eventually, either she'll move out on her own, or else Rose will decide she's ready to sell and will ask her to leave so she can sell to me. Because Rose *will* sell to me. There's no way she'd choose to sell that house to anybody else, especially since she knows that money is no object to me.

"It's crush season," Pam says. "I'll be at the vineyard tomorrow. Will I see you there?"

"You can count on it," I tell her. "I know how important it is to have all hands on deck right now. Plus, your dad always opens a few premium bottles at the end of a hard day's work, and I certainly wouldn't want to miss out on *that*."

"Are you more into reds or whites?" she asks.

"Both, depending on circumstance," I say. "But after a harvest, I'd go for something cold and crisp."

She grins. "All right," she says. "I guess you're not a complete novice."

"Oh, trust me, I've put a lot of time and energy into developing my opinions about wine. I'll tell you more sometime."

"Tomorrow, maybe," she offers. "Since we'll be seeing each other then."

"Sounds like a plan."

She glances out at the water. "I'm going to stay out here for a while, I like my early morning walks when it's cool and quiet," she says.

I take the hint. "You probably want to be alone. That's cool. I'll head back now. Sorry, I charged out here the way I did."

"Sorry, I was so hostile to you."

We're both smiling, despite our words. This could have been an ugly start for us, but I can tell that's not how it's going to end up. Instead, things feel full of hope and promise. I feel twenty years younger, which I'm sure she's bringing out in me. I have memories of meeting good-looking girls and *knowing* that something exciting was about to start, but it hasn't been that way in a long time. Nowadays, when I meet a woman, we both know that things will probably only last a few nights at the most.

I don't get that feeling when I look at Pamela. I feel something else. Like we're at the start of something that's going to have a little more meat to it. That's probably because our lives are already overlapping in so many ways. There's no way that whatever this is, is going to be a one-night stand.

To be honest, because of that, I probably shouldn't let it be anything at all. I should keep my distance from her. God knows Matt wouldn't like the idea that I'm fantasizing about the things I'd like to do with his daughter. He would throw me off his property and never let me come back.

But what Matt doesn't know won't hurt him, and it feels too late now to get her out of my head. She's taken up residence there for now.

Suddenly, I'm looking forward to the start of crush season a whole hell of a lot more than I was when I got up this morning.

Chapter 2
Pamela

The house is everything I dreamed it would be.

It's small, but not too small—three bedrooms, one of which I can use as an office, two full bathrooms, and a kitchen with brand-new appliances. The sliding glass doors in the master bedroom open directly onto the beach, which is where I'm standing now, gazing out at the lake, watching the surf crash against the familiar shore. It's good to be home.

I've had my eye on this place forever, ever since I was a kid. The fact that this house is right alongside the back of my family's vineyard makes it an ideal place for me to live—and, frankly, it also makes me feel as if I *should* own it. I used to imagine that it would be a fun place to have a secret club. Now, though, all I want is to make it my own. Renting is great, but I want this house to be mine. And as soon as I can convince Rose Crawford that it's in her best interest to sell to me, that dream will come true.

For now, though, I'm happy to be here. I'm excited to tell Dad about everything I learned at the University of Padova, the school in Padua where I've spent the last year. I'm excited to forget all about that prick Jean-Luc. It's not like I was taking my French fling all that seriously, but I didn't anticipate that he would ghost me three weeks before I was due to return to the US. I thought the two of us were going to make the most of all the time we had together. I had no idea I was the only one who felt that way about it.

Now, standing on the beach, I close my eyes and remember the warm, carefree nights with him in Padua. The way his hand used to graze my lower back when we were in public, with a touch that was almost possessive and hinted at everything he would do to me the moment we were alone together. The way he'd growl things I couldn't understand in my ear in French when we had sex—I speak French, and after a year in Padua I like to think I'm pretty good at it, but Jean-Luc could always keep me guessing. He would never tell me what it was he was saying, but by the smirk on his face every time I asked the question, I'm guessing it was probably pretty filthy.

My phone rings in my pocket, and I'm relieved. Dwelling on memories of Jean-Luc is no way to transition back to being at home. I pull the phone out of my pocket and see the photo I took last summer of my brother, Brian, lighting up the screen.

I can't keep a smile off my face as I answer the call. "Wondered when I was going to hear from you," I say in greeting.

"You're back in the States? When did you get home?" Brian demands.

"Last night," I tell him. "I'm all moved in and the house is gorgeous. I can't wait for you to see it."

"Rose still isn't open to selling, though?"

"She will," I say. "I have to convince her, that's all, but she'll sell to me eventually. Our family belongs in this house, we practically grew up here. She'll realize that."

"I hope you're right," Brian says. "It does seem like the perfect place for you. And I know you don't want to live in the big house anymore."

"Neither do you," I point out.

Brian laughs. "True enough," he says. "But I'm not sure buying a camper and parking it on the property is the right solution for you. You're a little fancier than I am."

"I am not *fancy*," I retort. But he's right. Brian's camper life - or should say *glamper* life - is not for me. I need things like air conditioning and a big bathtub to relax in at the end of a long day. Maybe I am a *little* fancy.

"How's New York?" I ask him.

"Exhausting," he says.

"Make any good deals?"

"Several five-star restaurants here will start stocking our cab sav, and a chain called "Memories" just added five more of our 2023 varietals."

"Hey, that's cool," I say. "When will you be home?"

"In a few weeks, I think."

"I hope you get back soon," I tell him. "I've missed you."

"What have you been up to?"

"Met the neighbor."

"We have a neighbor?" he asks, surprised at the fact. "In the mansion? I thought that was unoccupied."

"Well, it's occupied now. Maybe he moved in recently or something." I bite my thumbnail. "He says he volunteers at the vineyard sometimes. He knows Dad. His name's Christos."

"Wait. Seriously? You mean Chris, Chris Tzavaras?"

"Maybe. I don't remember his last name. It was something like that."

"Well, that's got to be him...he lives next door to you?"

"You know him?"

"Yeah, I know him. I've seen him working at the vineyard. I thought he was a drifter or a tourist or something, but we've become great friends. He is very smart, tells great stories, and is a quick study."

"Why would you think he was a drifter?"

"Because he keeps disappearing. For weeks at a time sometimes. He's only been around about," he paused, thinking. "Well, shortly after you left, but he's incredibly inconsistent. Of course, no one cares—Dad's glad for the free help, however, he can get it. But I don't understand why he'd keep vanishing if he lives that close by in that big old mansion."

"I don't know," I say. "I only met him today. But he seems a little...hard to get along with."

"Nah, Chris is all right," Brian says. "A little set in his ways, maybe, but good company once you get to know him."

I ponder that. Maybe my new neighbor and I can find a way to have a smooth relationship. "I'll see you when you get home," I tell my brother.

"Take care of Dad until I get back."

I end the call and tuck my phone back into my pocket. Coming home would be better if Brian was here. We grew up on the vineyard together and the place doesn't feel quite right without him. I'll feel more settled when I see Dad later, though. At least I've always got him here to make this place feel like home.

God, I can't wait to tell him everything I've learned. All the new ideas I have. Like my Camp and Learn program, which came to me while I was walking around in the heart of Padua—that'll be a perfect way to introduce wines to more people and spread awareness of our brand. Or the new varietals I want to try to create by crossing different grapes with one another. And then there's my idea to expand our tasting room into a high-end restaurant, complete with a five-star chef. That'll be a big change for us, but I think we can pull it off, and if we can, it will make our vineyard the dominant label in the Northern Lake Michigan area. I think Dad's going to love these ideas. He's going to be so glad he sent me to France. It's going to be great to tell him all about it.

In the meantime, I'm left pondering what happened with my new neighbor. *Christos*. It's wild to think that he works for Dad—or *volunteers* for Dad, as he says. It makes it harder for me to think of him as an extreme hottie.

Harder, but not impossible. I'm not blind, and I didn't miss those abs when he confronted me on the beach with his shirt unbuttoned and flapping in the breeze. If he wasn't a friend of Dad's, I might go over to his house tonight with a bottle of wine and see what I could make of the situation—but I can't do that. It would make things way too complicated.

Or would it? He *was* friendly on the beach. Nothing like he was when I first encountered him on my way out there... And those big blue eyes are enough to lose myself in their mesmerizing spell.

I had been walking along the path to the shore alongside my house. It was early, quiet, and serene, and I was thinking how nice it would be to set up a bench out here so I could relax and do some reading when a voice called out to me from above. "Hey!"

It took me a minute to locate the source of the yell. Finally, I saw him—a man with dark, wavy hair, bright eyes, and a five o'clock shadow, with a thin linen button-down shirt that left his torso tantalizingly exposed, was leaning out the upper window of the three-story house next to mine. My neighbor looked downright pissed off, making me wonder what the hell his problem was. It was a nice day out. I couldn't think of any reason to act the way he was.

Of course, that was before I met Christos. Now I think that might be his personality.

"Can I help you?" I called up to him.

He glowered down at me. "What the hell are you doing on my property?"

"On your property?" I looked around.

"That's my path you're walking on."

"Doesn't this path belong to my house?" I glanced over my shoulder at the property behind me. I knew this path belonged to me because the gate that led me to it is in my yard. This guy was fooling no one.

If anything, his scowl only deepened. "That's not your house."

"Okay," I called back to him and rolled my eyes. "You have a nice day."

Of course, the house *isn't* mine, well—not technically. Officially, it still belongs to Rose Crawford. So maybe that's what he meant. I'll convince Rose to sell, though, I'm sure of that, and then I'll have full rights to this place, and there won't be anything my grouchy, window-leaning spy of a neighbor can do about it.

I've been looking forward to coming home ever since I found out that Rose will rent her house to me. I've been yearning to live there for as long as I can remember. Near enough to the family winery that I'll be able to be a part of the daily goings-on, but far enough away to serve as my own private space...it's perfect, exactly what I need. But a cantankerous neighbor will mess all that up for me. The thought of him up in that window, watching my every move, glaring at me when I do something he doesn't like, runs the risk of souring the whole homecoming for me—but at least he's good-looking. Oh, that's an understatement, he is so fucking hot, that I happily let my mind undress him as we spoke. So there's always that.

I left my frustration behind as I came to the end of the path and stepped out onto the beach again. Only a small cove is visible from the balcony outside my bedroom. But now I'm looking at the whole huge expanse of Lake Michigan. It's breathtaking to stand beside a lake so big that it might as well be an ocean. With an expanse of water this size, I get lost in the sounds and breeze, and the soft sand beneath my feet. Other than the crisp fresh air scent of fresh water vs salt water you can't tell the difference.

France is beautiful, but there is no place like home.

I wandered along the shore, thinking I would make my way around the perimeter of the little peninsula and enjoy the ambiance. A part of me is wishing I'd brought a bottle out with me—something nice, something I wouldn't ordinarily open. I'm due for a celebration. But I'll do that later. The little beach in front of my house is the perfect spot for a bonfire, and for today I was happy to walk and listen to the lap of the waves against the shore.

But all too soon, thoughts of my neighbor began to make their way into my mind.

I mean, what was his problem? So, he didn't realize someone had moved into the house next to his, but it didn't take rocket science to figure out what was going on, surely. And why was his response to yell at me the way he did? What did he think, that I was trespassing or something? Even if I *had* been, was it such a big deal that he needed to yell out to me like that? I would have been off the path in a matter of minutes anyway. He could have let it go.

I sat down on the sand and frowned, looking out at the water.

I don't know. Maybe the best move would be to bake him some bread and take a bottle of wine over there. Make an overture of friendship - or other things.

On the other hand, why should I go out of my way to do that when he's the one who made things unfriendly in the first place?

These were the thoughts running through my head when I looked down the beach and saw a figure moving toward me, coming from the direction of my house. It didn't take long for me to figure out who I was looking at. That dark hair and stocky build, the aggression in the way he was walking—it was my angry neighbor, and he was coming over to confront me.

I couldn't believe the audacity. What the hell was his problem?

I got to my feet and brushed the sand off my pants, bracing for his arrival. If he wanted a confrontation, he was going to get one.

Or so I thought at the time.

Now I'm sitting in my house, doing what I can to face the fact that I didn't successfully confront him. I didn't tell him to leave me alone. If anything, I befriended him.

I still have no idea whether or not that was a good idea but it feels like there's no going back now. It's going to get very interesting.

Chapter 3
Pamela

A day spent picking grapes in the hot August sun is enough to wear anybody out. This would have been rough on me at the best of times. As it is, I've spent the past year as an academic rather than someone who works in a vineyard. I haven't done manual labor in ages. I'm not prepared for how strenuous the day has been, and by noon I'm worn out.

I'm expecting Christos to say something judgmental when he comes up and sees me sitting in the shade drinking ice water. The truth is, I'm embarrassed at having burned out so early, and there's a part of me that wants to go into the house and recover there so no one sees me resting. The college students Dad hires for the summer aren't having this problem. They haven't even taken their lunch break yet. And Christos, who is older than I am and should have hit his breaking point long before I did, doesn't even look like he broke a sweat.

He looks me over. "You okay?"

"I'm okay," I say, only partially honestly. "I'm hydrating, that's all. The heat. I'm fine."

"Yes, you are," he agrees with a sly grin.

Did I hear that right? Is he flirting with me?

"It's one of our hotter summers. Your face is red."

My red face is more likely caused by my blushing than the heat, but I have no idea how to tell him that. I decide I don't have to. "I'll be okay once I drink some water," I say.

"I think you should go inside and take advantage of the air conditioning."

"I was thinking about doing that," I admit.

"Well, let's go," he says.

"Let's?"

He shrugs. "You can give me a tour of the place. In all the time I've been helping your dad, I've never been inside the house. I wouldn't mind seeing it."

I have to wonder if there's a reason for that. I know Dad doesn't usually let employees into the house—he's always liked to keep a boundary between professional relationships and personal ones, and he says inviting people inside would breach that boundary. He puts out food and drinks for the people who work here, but it's always on folding banquet tables outside, never in the house. He doesn't even have them come into the outbuildings that are publicly a part of the vineyard, like the wine cellar that we open for tours or the tasting room unless there's some big fancy event going on.

But this is different, right? Christos isn't an employee. He's a volunteer—and more to the point, he's Dad's friend. At least, I think friends are what they are. To be honest, I'm not entirely clear on the nature of their relationship.

I can give him a tour though, I decide. "Sure," I say, getting up from the bench where I've been sitting.

But I stand up too fast. My head swims, I see stars, and my knees start to buckle. I feel his arm slide around my waist, heating my whole body. "Whoa," he says, holding me against him. "You good?"

"I'm good." My head's already clearing and I shake off the feigned electricity flowing through me. "I got up too fast, that's all."

"Do you want me to get your dad?"

"Definitely not." I say. Christos might not be planning to give me a hard time for the fact that my stamina isn't where it was last summer, but Dad definitely would. I grew up in this vineyard, and the fact that I can't keep up with the mid-August harvesting is more than a little embarrassing—it's not a problem I ever imagined I would have. Dad did tease me about this when I said I was going to France to study for a year. He told me if I spent too much time with my nose in books, I wouldn't be able to pull my weight with the grapes. I guess he was right about that.

I pull away from Christos and stand up so he'll know that I'm all right. I do feel better now—it was a momentary thing. "Let's go inside," I say. "I'll show you the house."

I can't shake the feeling, as we walk through the front door, that this action is full of significance somehow. Even though we're not going to do anything more than walk around my father's house, it feels more important than that. It feels like I've made a monumental decision. I don't know what's making me feel that way, but I can't deny it.

"Nice place," Christos comments. It's not the response I was expecting, to be perfectly honest. I know this house is more than *nice*. The little cottage I'm trying to buy from Rose Crawford is *nice*. This place is magnificent. When I was a kid and I'd bring friends home to play, they'd always have some comment about how big the house was, and eventually, I started feeling embarrassed about it.

It's a little bit of a relief that Christos isn't making a big deal out of it.

But then, I saw his house, and it's as big as this one is. Maybe this isn't such a big deal to him.

"What do you want to see?" I ask him, thinking he's going to ask for a tour of Dad's private cellar or something. I don't think Dad would approve—he's *very* particular about who he takes down there—but my heart is beating wildly, and I'm carried away with the excitement of the moment. Despite myself, I think I might do anything Christos asked me to right now. That's a heady feeling.

He leans in, and in a voice barely above a whisper, says "Show me the bedroom.".

I swear, my heart stops beating for a second.

I couldn't have heard him right, so I look up at him to make sure. "What?"

"You must have a bedroom in this house, right?" he says, his voice still low and sultry. "You grew up here."

"That's right," I say, clearing my throat of the breath that keeps catching there.

"Can I see it?"

His meaning isn't subtle at all. He doesn't want to see my childhood bedroom out of idle curiosity. I know exactly why he wants to go there. The truth is, I've been thinking about it too, ever since the moment we met on the beach, and then when he helped steady me outside. I could say no, of course. He's given me the window. It wouldn't even have to be awkward. I could make up some reason why we shouldn't go to the bedroom. I could lie and say it was Brian's room now. And I can tell that Christos would accept that. He wouldn't push me.

I can say no. But, I don't want to.

I swallow hard, barely able to believe what I'm about to do—but the idea of sending him away is more than I can fathom. I'm hyper-aware of his body and of how desperately attracted to him I am.

"Follow me," I manage.

We don't say a word on the way to my room, but I have never been so aware of another person's body in all my life. Even though he's behind me and I can't see him, I feel like I'm registering every move he makes. This walk is interminable. I feel like my blood is on fire.

What happens when we stop walking?

I get my answer the moment we cross the threshold into my room. He kicks the door shut behind him and throws the deadbolt, and I have a split second to feel grateful for the fact that I asked Brian to help me install that bolt when I was a teenager desperate for privacy. At least I know no one will be walking in on us.

I barely have time to finish that thought before Christos is on me. He wraps his arms around me, pulls me tight against his body, and kisses me with a fervor that I don't think I've ever experienced in my life.

I meet him with equal passion. It feels like we can't get close enough to each other. I've never felt this before—this wild desire to merge my body with someone else's. Sex has never been this *hot*. There's always been a sense of rationality, a bit of distance.

Today there's no distance. I *am* the primal urge to let this man fuck me senseless, and if I had to name something else about myself, I don't think I could do it right now.

Our clothes are coming off fast, and I don't even fully realize it's happening until he lowers his mouth to my nipple and flicks his tongue against it. Pleasure sparks through me and I gasp, arching my back to grant him better access and wondering when the hell he took my bra off. I don't care, though. I work my thumbs into the waistband of my panties and shove them down. Now I'm fully naked and it still isn't enough. I want to put myself on display for him. I want to spread myself open for him.

He picks me up off the floor and gently moves me backward onto the bed, where I land with a light bounce. All I can do is stare at him as he approaches. He pulls his shirt over his head and tosses it aside, revealing a sparsely hairy, well-muscled torso. I inhale sharply. I didn't even know I was into men built like this, but I can't imagine ever going back to a lanky Parisian now.

He shucks off his pants and all I can do is stare shamelessly. His cock is *massive*. It's a little intimidating, and at the same time, it feels like a challenge I'm dying to take on. I've never had anyone anywhere near that big. I want – no, need – to know what he feels like.

He stands before me, with a huge erection, full, bare, and unabashed, his confidence filling the room like a potent fragrance. The dim light dances over his taut skin, tracing the contours of his muscles as he moves closer. I can't tear my gaze away from the mesmerizing intensity in his eyes; they are dark and full of want, and I know they reflect my desire. His hands reach out, finding the curve of my waist, and his touch is electric, sending shivers through my body.

With deliberate slowness, he leans in and captures my lips in a searing kiss. His mouth is warm and demanding, igniting a fire within me. He pulls away from the kiss, leaving me gasping and wanting more, my lips tingling from his touch. His hands glide over my skin, exploring every curve and contour with a mix of reverence and lust. His fingers trace lines of fire along my body, awakening every nerve and leaving a trail of goosebumps in their wake.

My senses are overwhelmed by the taste of him, the heat of his skin, and the strength of his grip as he pulls me closer, leaving no space between us. His touch is both rough and tender, stirring a primal longing that leaves me breathless. As we move together, the world fades away, and all that remains is the intoxicating dance of our bodies, driven by an undeniable hunger for each other.

He leans in again, his lips brushing against my neck as he whispers words I can barely hear, but their meaning sends a rush of heat through me. His teeth graze my skin, and I can't suppress a shiver of delight. His breath is warm against my ear as he kisses his way down my collarbone, igniting a burning anticipation within me. His touch is deliberate, each movement a calculated tease that leaves me craving more.

"I wonder what your father would say," he murmurs, "if he knew the things I'm about to do to his daughter."

That shouldn't sound so hot. But fuck, I love how dangerous and forbidden this feels. "Maybe we don't tell him," I manage. As I'm melting into his arms.

His grin is feral. "Sounds like a plan to me."

He crawls onto the bed and positions himself over me. He rocks his hips a few times, grinding his cock between my legs. I want to fuck. I want it bad. But this friction is more than any hot-blooded woman could be expected to take. My legs are shaking with excitement as our bodies move together with a fluidity that feels natural yet extraordinary. Every touch and every caress is charged with desire, building a crescendo of pleasure that makes me dizzy with longing. His hands find mine, entwining our fingers as he pushes me further back onto the bed, his weight pressing against me in a way that feels both commanding and tender. We are lost in the intoxicating rhythm of our desires, each moment a symphony of sensation and emotion.

I try to tell him how close I am, how I'm about to come all over him, but I can't find the words. I'm falling apart.

But maybe he already knows. The moment my orgasm crashes into me, he shoves his way inside of me.

He was right to get me there first. The way he's stretching me out, filling me up—I think this would have hurt a little if I was in my right

FATHER'S BEST FRIENDS BABY

mind. I'm trying hard to hold back my screams of pleasure, and I can't imagine any pain being intense enough to break through the ecstasy I'm feeling right now.

By the time I start to come down, my body has adjusted enough that all I can feel is *want* and *more* and *fuck*, and I lift my hips to him again and again and watch the downright pornographic expression on his face as his climax builds. Seeing him like this is enough to get me going again. By the time his hand clenches around mine and he grunts out, "Pam, I'm close, I—" I'm on the verge again myself, and this time the two of us fall over the edge together, lips meeting in a kiss and swallowing one another's screams.

As our breaths gradually slow and our bodies calm, we find ourselves in a cocoon of serenity. The rush of passion ebbs, leaving us blissful in a sense of deep contentment. His strong arms encircle me, holding me close, and I nestle against his chest, savoring the comforting rhythm of his heartbeat beneath my cheek. His skin is warm and slightly damp, a tangible reminder of our shared experience.

He strokes my hair with gentle fingers, a soothing gesture that lulls me into a peaceful daze. His touch is unhurried and tender, a quiet promise of safety and care. I close my eyes, feeling a sense of quiet intimacy wash over us, a connection that seems to deepen with every passing moment.

We lay there in silence, the only sound the soft hum of our breathing and the occasional rustle of the sheets. I can feel the weight of his gaze on me, and when I open my eyes, his are filled with a warmth that feels as though it could melt away any remaining barriers between us. He smiles softly, a silent assurance that he is here, present in this moment with me.

I return his smile, feeling an overwhelming sense of gratitude for the intimacy we've created. Our bodies are intertwined, and as I breathe in the scent of him, I know that this moment is something to be cherished. Wrapped in his arms, I allow myself to drift into a state of quiet bliss, savoring the gentle embrace of the man beside me.

It is the hottest thing I've ever experienced in my life. And as we begin to cool down and gradually separate from one another, the only thing I can say for certain is that, while I can't quite piece together what brought us to this point, we're definitely going to do that again.

Chapter 4
Christos

I have no idea how I'm going to face Matt today, after what happened between me and Pam yesterday.

Hell, I wasn't even planning that. I mean, don't get me wrong, I am not having regrets. It was one of the hottest things I've ever experienced in my life. I'd been fantasizing about her since we met on the beach, and the reality definitely exceeded all my daydreams—and how often can you say *that* about a hookup? Not that often, in my case. Possibly never before, in fact.

But I did think it would be awkward to be around Matt today while thoughts of his naked daughter ran on replay through my head. So I'm relieved to get to the vineyard and find out he isn't there.

"He's taking an important meeting with some bigwig in town," says Robbie, one of the college volunteers. "He did leave instructions, though. We're supposed to be picking the pinot noir today."

I nod. That's what I figured we would be doing. Matt uses his pinot grapes to make a sparkling wine, and it's important to harvest them early so they don't turn overly sugary. I grab a basket, relieved at this turn of luck. I'll be able to lose myself in the work, and I won't have to worry about coming face to face with Matt and what I'm going to say to make things seem normal when we see each other.

I was so worried about facing Matt, though, that I didn't even think about the other, very obvious dilemma. I find her after about an hour, balancing a basket full of grapes on her hip. Her back is to me, and for a moment I let myself enjoy the sight of her in her skintight shorts and crop top. She looks like she's dressed for yoga or something. I wonder if this is what she wears into the orchard when her father *is* home.

I wonder if this is what she's wearing because she knew I would be here. Ooh, that's a hot idea. I can see the entire shape of her body in that outfit. She's covered up, but she might as well be naked, because if I squint and look at her silhouette, I can imagine she is.

Not that I need to be doing that right now.

She turns and glances over at me, flashing a smile. "Hey," she says.

That's all. *Hey*. But it feels full of meaning. I'm positive she's thinking about what went on between us every bit as much as I am, and I don't feel like I even need to ask her whether she wants it to happen again. The answer is in the energy and tension between the two of us. If I hadn't felt sure that we were eventually going to hook up again, that smile she's giving me and that single word would have done the job.

And it takes all the pressure off. I don't need to seduce her. I don't have to win her over. She's right there with me.

I start to pick the grapes alongside her. It feels strangely innocent, even though the air between the two of us is still boiling, and I guess I like that. It's been a while since things have felt this innocent between me and a woman, like we could have a conversation without any agenda. And it's not as if I don't have an agenda, of course. It's the fact that I feel like my agenda has already been achieved—that's why I'm not feeling any pressure here.

"You seem like you're feeling better," I comment.

She darts a quick glance at me, probably to see whether I'm making fun of her, which I'm not. I've been working here long enough that I've seen plenty of people gas out in the heat of summer. It's about ten degrees cooler today, thankfully, so I don't think we're at risk of that. Although I almost find myself wishing we were – it would be a good excuse to take her into the house. Inside the house is a lot more fun than outside, that's for sure.

She seems to decide she isn't being mocked. "I'm glad the temperature went down a bit," she says. "It makes it a lot easier to work out here."

"I'm sure we'll see more cases of heat exhaustion this summer."

Pam gives me an indignant look. "I didn't have heat exhaustion."

"I mean, it's fine if you did, though. It was ninety-five degrees out and we were working in the sun all day. It could have happened to anybody."

She sighs and rakes a hand through the front of her hair, which only serves to loosen the braid hanging down her back. A few strands of hair come free and fall around her face, framing it prettily.

I'm in conflict. A part of me is thinking how sweet she looks and another part of me is thinking about what it would be like to fuck her with that braid in her hair. From behind, maybe. Holding onto it. Oh, hell.

"I guess I feel embarrassed about it, that's all," she says. "I know I need to build up my stamina again after spending a whole year in libraries and air-conditioned restaurants. I should have expected that I wouldn't have the same tolerance for heat as I used to."

"I mean, it is Michigan," I say. "That extreme degree of heat isn't exactly the standard around here, even in the middle of August."

"Yeah," Pam agrees. "It was...an unusually hot day."

I let her comment hang in the air. I can tell she means it in exactly the way I'm taking it, and rather than spoil the moment by calling it out, I'm content to sit inside the innuendo. It feels something like a promise of things to come.

Pam is the one who breaks the silence, clearing her throat. "Do you want to hang around after we're done for the day?" she asks.

I raise my eyebrows, wondering what *hang around* might mean.

Pam laughs. "I was thinking of opening a bottle of Dad's special reserve," she explains. "It'll be better with someone to share it with, that's all."

"Oh," I say, not sure if I'm disappointed. Obviously, I want to get with her again, but right now it seems so apparent that that's going to happen that the idea of waiting is more tantalizing somehow. Letting the tension build—that's not something I usually do with women, simply because we're not in each other's lives for that long. I like the idea of doing it with her.

"You don't have to," Pam says, mistaking my hesitation for something other than what it is.

"No, I'd like to," I clarify. "I think it would be a lot of fun. And Matt's never let me into his special reserve."

"Yeah, I'm not supposed to either," she says. "He's a bit of a hoarder about it. He always says he'll open a bottle when there's a special occasion, but there never seems to be a special occasion. He isn't going to miss one."

"Fair enough."

"And if he does catch us, we'll tell him the whole thing was my idea," she quips.

I laugh. "It *was* your idea," I remind her. "But you don't need to take the fall here. I can handle Matt."

She chuckles. "I can handle him too," she reminds me. "I've been doing it all my life."

The rest of the day goes by easily and pleasantly. I always feel relaxed when I'm working in the vineyard—that's why I volunteer to do it. But today is even more relaxing than a normal day. I'm able to completely forget about the things that normally occupy my mind—thoughts about work, for example, and worries about business deals I'm trying to close. Today all that matters is the rich, fruity aroma of the grapes around me, the anticipation of a bottle of wine at the end of the day, and the sexy woman working next to me, who keeps stealing glances at me and grinning shiftily, reminding me that the two of us are in together on a delicious secret.

Eventually, it gets too dark to continue working. The rest of the team packs up and heads out for the day, and then it's only me and Pam, alone together. She wipes her forehead with a bandana and smiles at me. "Come on."

"Where are we going?"

"The tasting room."

I've never been in Matt's tasting room before. I know he hosts events there, and I could have gone, but I haven't felt the need. He always brings bottles out to me when he wants to offer me something. But Pam is practically bouncing up and down with excitement as she leads me in. "This is my favorite place on the property," she explains. "Ever since I was a little girl I've loved coming here."

"You couldn't have had much to do in a wine-tasting room as a little kid, though," I comment.

She flips on the overhead lights and I take the place in as she walks ahead and behind the bar. There are standing tables and low tables with chairs around them. The entire back wall is racks and racks of wine bottles, and there's a long counter spread in front of that. I see little stemless glasses for tasting, but Pam ignores those and pulls down two of the stemmed glasses that are hanging from an overhead mount. She puts them down on the counter, bends down, and brings up a bottle from underneath.

She shows it to me. "It's a Shiraz," she says. "I know it's not labeled. Dad doesn't put the labels on these until he's about to sell them. It's a weird quirk of his."

"What's it like?"

"Astonishingly full-bodied," she says expertly. "A real cavalcade of flavors. Incredibly earthy, but plummy as well—see for yourself."

She grabs a corkscrew and opens the bottle. I watch her pour dexterously, looking as if she's done this a million times in her life. It's alluring to watch her—she's so skilled at this. I guess it's the combination of having grown up on the vineyard and her French education. She is very good at what she does.

She hands me one of the glasses and swirls the other one slowly, releasing the flavor of the wine. I do the same. I'm used to being the most knowledgeable person about wine and how to drink it in any room I'm in—provided Matt isn't there, of course, because no one matches him when it comes to this stuff. His daughter, though might give us both a run for our money.

We sip from our glasses at the same time.

I'm blown away. No wonder Matt doesn't like to open these bottles—this is genuinely the best Shiraz I've ever tasted. I don't even like Shiraz all that much, but this one is knocking my socks off. I'm going to need the entire glass to fully appreciate all the different notes of flavor it contains.

"Good, right?" Pam asks.

"Amazing," I tell her, and it's the truth. "You guys could make a fortune selling this stuff."

"This is only the beginning," she says.

"What do you mean?"

"I'm hoping to add to the varietals we grow this season. Start a new crop. Right now we've got the Pinot, the Shiraz, and the Riesling, but

FATHER'S BEST FRIENDS BABY

I want to introduce some less common, more artisan types. That's part of what I've been studying."

I nod, sipping again. It all sounds fascinating, like something I would be interested in even if I wasn't here with a sexy woman I was hoping to fuck. Even if we were only going to be friends, I'd want to know more about what she's talking about.

And that fact, if such a thing were even possible, makes me want to get naked with her even more.

I can already tell that this summer is going to be the most exciting one I've had in a while.

Chapter 5
Pamela

"How was the meeting?" I ask Dad.

He sighs. "I don't know that I want to get into it over dinner," he says. "This is our first time going out to eat together since you got back. Can't we keep things nice?"

"Oh, no. That means it wasn't good."

"It didn't go the way we hoped it would," he admits.

"Are we not getting the land?"

The land in question is a huge parcel to the north of our existing vineyard, and it's going to be instrumental in realizing the vision that Dad and I share for MacLaine Wines. I'm aching to introduce some rare international varietals to our crop. It would set us apart from any other growers in the region, and we'd be able to make a name for ourselves in a way we've only dreamed of doing so far. I've been beyond excited about it ever since I spoke to Dad on the phone from France and he agreed that it was the logical next step for us. And now that I'm home, it's time for us to get things underway.

That's why he was meeting with Harrison Cooper the other day, while Christos and I were drinking his reserve Shiraz. And tonight's dinner was *supposed* to be about him telling me what happened in that meeting. It's not like I'm interrupting what's meant to be a pleasant family dinner to talk business. This was supposed to be about business.

It worries me that he doesn't want to talk about it now.

"Dad," I say, putting down my fork, "you've got to tell me what happened. It's not like you're going to be able to keep it to yourself, you know. Eventually, I'm going to find out."

Dad sighs. "I don't think we're going to be able to buy that land, kid," he says.

"Why not?" I don't understand. "I thought it was for sale."

"Yeah, it is for sale."

"So then what's the problem?" I ask. "Don't tell me Cooper changed his mind about wanting to sell."

Cooper pulling the sale doesn't make sense, but after my problems with Rose Crawford as I try to buy the beach house, I can admit that I'm a little skeptical about property owners' willingness to part with their land.

"He's selling," Dad says heavily. "I don't think we can afford it, that's all."

"What do you mean?" I ask. That doesn't make sense at all. "We've been working on this for months. We've been to the bank, we've gotten the land appraised...we *can* afford it. We've been over the numbers dozens of times."

"I know," Dad says. "But Cooper says he's got an offer from another buyer."

"Another buyer?" I frown. That's not good. That land is perfect for growing grapes. If someone else is trying to buy it, that means we've got a competitor. And we do have competitors in the area, of course—other families with vineyards nearby—but to try to buy land that backs right up against ours is pretty low. I wouldn't have thought any of them capable of a move like that. It's aggressive and borderline personal, like they're trying to take us specifically out of business. God knows we wouldn't have done it to any of them.

"Who's the buyer?" I ask Dad.

"Don't know," Dad says.

"Cooper wouldn't tell you?"

"I wouldn't have asked him to. It'd be unethical."

"Dad, this is no time to worry about *ethics,* for God's sake. Someone's trying to put us under!" I shout, getting emotional at the thought of our family business being attacked.

"That doesn't mean we can put Cooper in a compromising position," Dad says patiently. "It's not his fault he got another offer, and I can't blame him for wanting the best price."

"But we have to know who's doing this if we're going to stop them," I protest.

"I know," Dad says calmly. "I get that. And I'm going to do everything I can to find out who's behind it. But I can't do that by forcing Cooper to tell me. None of this is his fault, and it wouldn't be fair to him to put him in that position."

I have to hand it to my father. I'm not worried about doing right by Harrison Cooper right now. I want to go to war with whoever is trying to take away our dream. But Dad has never been anything short of responsible and upstanding. I shouldn't have imagined he'd breach ethics, even in a situation like this one. Of course he wouldn't.

But then what's the plan? "How are you going to find out what's going on?" I ask him.

"I'll go to some of the other families that own vineyards around here," he says. "I'll ask them."

"You think they're going to tell you?"

"It's not the type of thing that would stay a secret for long, even if they didn't want to tell me," he points out. "The moment someone acquires that land and starts growing, it's going to be obvious who it is. I'm guessing whoever is doing this *wants* us to know about it. They aren't buying up that property right behind ours because they're going for subtlety."

He's got a point, but even so... "What if they won't tell you anything? I might not if it was me. I might want to keep it to myself until I was sure the deal had gone through."

"I don't know who taught you to be so conniving," Dad laughs.

"*You* did," I tell him. My dad might be ethical, but that doesn't mean he's not a strategic entrepreneur, and yeah, I learned everything I know from him. I wouldn't have said it was conniving, though. I would have said strategic, or innovative, or even passionate. I wouldn't even blame the other growers if they didn't want to tell us what they were up to right now—why on Earth would they?

"We know a few more things," Dad says. "We know the amount of the other offer. We can surmise who would be capable of making a deal like that because it's not an amount that everyone would be able to come up with."

"What do you mean?" I ask him. "How much is it?

When he names the sum, I don't mean to, but I gasp. "Are you serious?" I ask him, my jaw nearly resting on the table. "Who's paying that amount of money for that land?"

"Well, that's the question," Dad agrees. "I don't know. That's what we've got to find out."

"That's more than twice what we were offering," I say, still shocked.

"I know. And we weren't trying to get an unfair deal or anything. We offered the value of the property according to the appraisal we had done. That's what gets at me. Someone is paying more—considerably more—than what this land is worth."

"Someone would go to that much trouble to target us as competition?"

"I guess so, " he says, shaking his head in disbelief. "I know it sounds crazy."

"Is someone out there angry with us? I don't understand," I admit. We have business rivals, of course, as everyone does. But this is not a good business decision. This seems extremely personal. Why would anyone pay twice as much as the land was worth unless their sole purpose was to take it away from us?

But I can't understand why anyone would want to take it away from us. I wasn't aware that any rival growers disliked us on a personal level, and yet I have no idea how else to interpret this. It's alarming.

Dad shakes his head. "I wish I had a better answer," he says. "I have no idea why someone would want to buy that land at such a high price. I agree with you—it does seem like they're trying to take it from us. But I'm as lost as you are when it comes to what their reason could be."

"And there's not even a chance we could counteroffer?" I already know this is hopeless even as I'm suggesting it. I've been a part of all the financial conversations. I know what we're capable of and what we aren't.

Sure enough, Dad shakes his head. "I was tempted for a moment to see about getting a loan," he says. "But even knowing your plans for new varietals, which I think are great, I don't think we can be confident that we'd make that large a sum of money back quickly enough to get ourselves out of the hole."

He's probably right, of course, but it's devastating. I can feel all the things I've been dreaming about slipping through my fingers. I had so many plans, and I *know* they were good ones. Now they're gone. No new varietals. No expanded tasting room. No fancy restaurant with a five-star chef to design a menu that pairs perfectly with our family's best wines. I was going to put MacLaine Wines on the map.

Now it feels a little like my time in France was all for nothing. Sure, I got an education, but if I can't put it to use, what was the point? It's like my relationship with Jean-Luc—fun in the moment, but a waste of my time in the end. And I can't get that year back, on either front.

"Hey, don't get upset," Dad says. "We're going to figure something out."

"There's no way we can buy that property."

"No, there isn't, but...that doesn't mean we have to let go of *all* your ideas. They're good ones. We can probably still build out the tasting room."

"What about the restaurant?"

"I'm not sure where we would put it," Dad admits. "We don't have the room for a restaurant on the property we have now. You know that."

I do know that. That's why I was so anxious to acquire extra property in the first place—because we need it to realize all these ideas I have in my mind. I appreciate Dad trying to reassure me that all isn't lost, but it feels like it is.

"You're right," I tell him. "We shouldn't have talked about it over dinner."

He sighs. "I know you're upset, kid," he says, covering my hand with his. "I am too. I genuinely loved all your ideas. I was very excited about putting them into action."

"I'm sorry," I say. "I don't mean to be negative about this."

"You're disappointed. It's alright to be."

"It's just that I *know* this would have worked. I know it. We would have taken our business to the next level. We'd be the premier winery in all of Michigan. And it's hard to let go of that idea. I can see it in my mind, you know?"

"I do know. Brian's going to be disappointed too," he says, playing the role of Dad more than the businessman now.

"I can't understand how you're not angry about someone buying us out like this."

"Who said I wasn't angry?"

"I don't know. You seem calm."

"Comes with age," he says, sipping his glass of ice water. My father may be a wine lover, but when we're out to dinner, it's always water for him, unless he's specifically out with wine on his mind. He tells me he wants to be careful not to overindulge for fear wine will become less special to him. Personally, that's not a problem I can imagine ever having. It's impossible to imagine my passion for wine dimming.

Maybe that's why I'm raging right now and he's calm. I'm a more intense person than he is. I can imagine Brian laughing at the suggestion, telling me it's cute that I think that's even up for debate, that I'm the hothead of the family. I wish Brian was home right now. He would have something to say about all of this that would probably put it in perspective if nothing else. And knowing him, he would find a way to make me feel like all my dreams hadn't died.

But he isn't here, I'll have to figure it out. I'll have to hope that Dad can find a way for us to buy that land somehow.

Right now, though, things aren't looking good.

Chapter 6
Christos

The phone call from Harrison Cooper comes in at o-seven-hundred sharp. Luckily for me, I'm already up and brewing my morning coffee. On some mornings, I wouldn't be out of bed this early. Benefits of being retired from active service—you can sleep in a little bit. Of course, my SEAL training lingers, and it's hard for me to sleep in, so as often as not I do find myself up and about earlier than I'd like to be.

I do want to take this call, though. I've been waiting for it. I answer the phone and start to pour the water over the coffee grounds, "Morning, Harrison."

"I'll be brief." Harrison always starts conversations like this—direct and to the point. It's something I appreciate about him, but it also makes me laugh. It's as if he thinks he's going to lose my attention if he takes more than a few minutes to explain himself, which of course he wouldn't. "I'm calling about the offer you made on the property," he says.

"I figured as much." I can't resist saying that. What else would he be calling about? "Are you accepting the offer?"

I feel a surge of excitement as I ask the question. I've had my eye on that patch of land since I moved here. Admittedly, that isn't that long, but it is longer than I'm used to having to wait to get the things I want. My prior experiences with property acquisition have usually been same-day affairs. There's not much you can't make happen if you're willing to throw enough money at the problem.

But Harrison hesitates.

"Probably," he says.

"Probably?" I'm a little staggered by that. "Don't tell me someone made you a better offer."

"There is another offer," he says.

"Well, I'll match it."

"No, no. Yours is the higher offer. And I'll almost definitely be selling to you, you don't need to worry. I don't think they can afford the amounts you're offering."

"So what's the problem?" I pour my coffee into my mug and take a slow sip. It's still too hot, but I need caffeine for this conversation. I want my mind sharp if we're going to be moving into negotiations, which we apparently are.

"I need to give the other buyer a chance to raise their offer," Harrison says.

"I thought you said they weren't going to be able to match mine."

"Well, no, I don't *think* they are. But I should at least give them the chance to try."

"I don't get it," I say blankly. "I'm offering you double what that land is worth. This should be open and shut."

"It'll be resolved quickly, I can promise you that much."

"Are you reluctant to sell to me personally?" I can't see why he would be, but I don't have any other explanation for this. Also, it's starting to become a bit of a disturbing pattern—people in this area not wanting to sell me the property I'm interested in. At this rate, I should probably be glad I was even able to buy my house.

"It's nothing personal against you," he assures me. "It's the other buyer. I have to consider what's right for them."

"I don't know what you're talking about. You'd sell to a buyer who was offering a lower price? That doesn't make sense. What reason could you have for that?"

"They own some land nearby," Harrison says. "That's what makes me think they might try hard to come up with an offer that will match yours. Are you familiar with the MacLaine Vineyard?"

"Oh shit." That stops me dead in my tracks. "The *MacLaines* are trying to buy this land?"

"Yes. And I can only imagine it means a lot to them. From a financial standpoint, I can't pull the plug on this too quickly. For all I know, they'll take out a massive loan to match what you're offering."

"Well, money is no object for me," I assure him. "If they make another offer, I'll top it."

"Oh, I do not doubt that," Harrison said. "And now you see why I will keep the negotiations open for a little longer."

He's right. I do see it now. I see it, and it annoys the hell out of me. Any inclination I had to feel guilty for the fact that I compete with Matt MacLaine over this piece of land flies away at the thought that he's delaying me from getting what I want. Of course, he doesn't know that…but for fucks' sake, he and I both know he can't afford to pay the price I can. He should have backed out immediately when Harrison told him there was another offer.

I do feel bad. But only a little bad. After all, Matt's already got a huge piece of property that he's using to make his business dreams come true. He's already the owner of a successful vineyard. And if he wants to expand, sure, there's a part of me that supports his ambitions. I consider him a friend at this point and he's always been decent to me. But at the same time—I want to open a vineyard too, and I don't already have one. I can't see why I should back off and let him have this land. He's doing fine.

"Well, get back to me when you have an answer from the MacLaines," I tell Harrison. "It's not going to make any difference. If they have a counteroffer, I'll beat it."

"If you want to save time, you could increase your offer right now," Harrison said. "I could take an even higher number back to them and it would probably scare them off."

Yeah, it probably would. But I'm annoyed by how this is going down, and right now I don't feel like offering Harrison Cooper more money than he's already getting. I'll do it if I have to—if it's either that or lose the land. But unless things come to that point, I won't pay him one dime more than I've already offered. Frankly, he's stringing me and Matt along by playing these games. This should have been over already.

"You can let me know when you've got their answer," I tell him again, letting a little acid creep into my voice this time. I don't mind him knowing I'm irritated with him. He's making things difficult for me.

I don't think he minds, because he doesn't drop the smug attitude when he answers. "You'll be hearing from me," he assures me. "Maybe a few more days. Feel free to reach out if you change your mind about increasing."

Yeah. He can keep dreaming, but that's not going to happen.

I take my coffee out onto the balcony. From here, I can look over and see Rose Crawford's beach house—or maybe I should call it Pam's beach house since she's the one who's living there. Speaking of things that are getting under my skin, having Pam in that house is creating all kinds of mixed feelings for me. On the one hand, I want to buy that house. I don't know what her long-term plans are—I can't imagine she intends to stay there for long, given that her father owns one of the biggest homes in the area. She can't *need* that little place. I'm sure this is a temporary situation for her.

And at the same time, the fact that she's so close all the time makes me a little crazy, because I could go over there any time I wanted. I could knock on her door and make a move, and most of the time I think exactly that. I don't know why I'm not doing exactly that.

All I can say is that the chemistry between us is so potent that I *know* something else will happen, and it feels like a mistake to manufacture that moment. As I imagine that instant, my mind races with thoughts of Pamela's intense gaze locking with mine, her lips parting in anticipation as she draws me in. The thought of her touch sends a shiver down my spine, I can hardly ignore my immediate physical response beneath my pants right now, as my firmness builds, pressing insistently against the inside of my shorts.

The anticipation heightens the tension in my body, as I imagine her fingertips tracing a slow, deliberate path across my skin, setting my nerves ablaze. The vision of us tangled in a passionate embrace, lost in each other, is enough to recognize I want her. My mind lingers on her touch.

It will be so much more arousing if I let it come to me.

Chapter 7
Pamela

Dinner with Dad lingers in my mind over the next few days. I can't believe this is happening. It seems like a bad dream. I was looking forward to introducing some of the rare varietals I've been learning about, expanding our tasting room, and planning the menu for the restaurant I want to open. And now none of that is going to happen. There's no chance.

I'm trying to be grateful for the things I do have. After all, we still own a great vineyard. There are still so many ways for me to put my education to use here. I'm one of the lucky ones. So my dreams aren't going to look exactly the way I hoped they would—I can adjust to that. I can get past it. It's okay.

But right now, it's a little soul-crushing.

I'm sitting on a rock that looks out over the water. The lake is calming at a time like this. It gives me something to focus on other than my problems, which is a nice break. Despite how things are going, I *am* happy to be home.

"Want company?"

Ah. The other reason I'm glad to be home. I look up at Christos and smile. When he's around, it's hard to remember what I saw in Jean-Luc, and I know that if the rest of my life presents me with choices between skinny French poets and muscular Greek men, that won't be any choice. It's clear to me now who's my right type.

"Take a seat," I invite him, sliding over on the rock. He perches on the edge and looks out at the water like he thinks he'll catch a glimpse of whatever I'm looking at. I can't tell him my thoughts are far away from this beach and the lake shore. I don't want to make him deal with the seriousness of that. He's my fuck buddy, not my confidante.

Besides, having him so close to me is already a better distraction than the view could ever hope to be. I relax my body and find that he's leaning forward enough that my back makes contact with his chest. He breathes in, and I rise and fall with him.

"Been thinking about you," he says, his voice so soft that I hardly hear him over the sound of the wind rushing around me. It's a warm night, and the wind is the only thing that makes being outside bearable, but suddenly I wish it would quiet down. I turn toward him, thinking maybe I'll hear him better that way.

The wind blows again and I get the scent of his body, spicy and sea-salty, and then, before I can even think about what I'm doing, I'm kissing him.

Oh *fuck,* it was worth waiting for. I'm grateful now that I put this moment off, and glad I didn't try to make something happen between us the other night when we opened that Shiraz. Letting the tension build was the right thing to do. I know at once how far this will go, and I also know we won't make it back to either of our houses. That wouldn't be true if we'd given in to each other more recently. I might have been more capable of waiting the time it takes to walk home. I might have been able to take my hands off of him long enough to get somewhere private.

The hell with it.

I climb into his lap and straddle him, wrapping my legs around him, already angry at the fact that we're both so overdressed. My jean shorts have never felt like such a burdensome amount of clothing before. I can feel him getting hard in a hurry as I roll my hips into his body, wanting more of him.

"Take your pants off," he breathes, his voice ragged.

"We're doing this here?" I want to. I want to so fucking bad. I never thought of myself as the exhibitionist type, but there is something so alluring about the knowledge that this is a public beach with only blades of seagrass shielding us. Anyone could come walking by at any moment. The fact that we need each other so badly that we can't even wait until we can get ourselves to a more private place makes this one of the hottest experiences I think I've ever had in my life. All I want are his hands on my body and to feel him inside me. I want to ride him until this craving is finally satisfied.

His hands slide up under the hem of my shirt, his thumbs gently play with my nipples, and I forget for a moment that there's anything I need to do to take this to the next level. All I care about are the sudden sparks of desire shooting through my whole body. I wrap my legs around his waist to bring us closer together.

"Hey," he says gruffly, removing his hands from my shirt. I moan at the loss. He reaches behind him, grabs my ankles, unlocks them, and pushes me gently off of him. "I said to take your pants off."

I slide down into the sand and do as he told me, feeling wild, dangerous, and vulnerable sitting exposed like this on the beach. Feeling shy, I pull my shirt down a little to cover myself.

He shakes his head. "Take that off too."

"Christos—"

"You wanted to do this here," he says, his voice shockingly low. "Show me you want it, if you do."

And, fuck, I would do *anything* he said if he said it in that voice. I pull my shirt over my head and toss it away.

He watches me for a moment, saying nothing, his eyes full of expectation, which is fair because I know what he wants now. All I'm wearing is my bra, and I shiver a little as I remove it. There is no going back now.

It's not what I imagined when I decided I wanted him to fuck me right out here on the beach. I figured I'd be at least partly dressed, that I'd have some manner of protection if anyone came wandering by. I didn't imagine being this exposed.

But—it's tantalizing. It's making the whole experience so much hotter, and I'll remember to thank Christos later, when I'm back in my right mind, for pushing me to my limits like this. He's taken me beyond what I thought I was capable of sexually, and this is only the second time.

I wonder what else I'd do.

Christos unbuckles his pants and pushes them down around his ankles. He's not taking all of *his* clothes off. I'm the only one who's buck naked on this beach. It's such a fucking power move that if I wasn't so eager for him to fuck me, I'd probably be mad at it.

"Get back over here," he says.

I move slowly back over to the rock, even though I want to race to him. I give him plenty of time to see what he's done, to take in the sight of me walking naked on this beach, something I never thought I would be bold enough to do. If this is happening, I'm not going to do it halfway. I'm going all out with it.

I balance myself with a hand on his shoulder as I climb back into his lap and position myself carefully over him. I lower my body enough that he's pressing against me, so he's barely inside me. I can hardly breathe for wanting him. I can feel the weight of his desire hanging in the air, palpable and electric. I meet his gaze, my heart racing with anticipation, and decide to tease him just a little. Two can play this enticing power game.

I stretch backward, savoring how his breath hitches in response. His need is tangible, but I want him to savor this moment of anticipation. My touch lingers on his skin for just a heartbeat longer, and then I pull away, watching the hunger intensify in his gaze. It's a delicious dance, this back-and-forth, and I can't wait to see how he responds when I finally let him come inside me. His eyes are dark with longing, and I revel in the power of it. I let a slow, wicked smile spread across my lips, a silent promise of what's to come.

"Pamela," he groans.

That's exactly what I wanted to hear—a little sign that I too have some control. It's enough to break my resolve, and I slide down on him, taking him fully inside me.

As we move together, he wraps his arms around me and holds me against his chest, and despite everything, I do feel sheltered. It feels like he's creating his own little space for the two of us, and even though we're hidden away on a public beach, I feel safe. I'm able to lose myself completely in the rhythm of our bodies, in the fullness of him moving inside me. He runs his fingers up and down the length of my spine and it's electrifying. I could do this for hours. Days.

I moan a little and increase the tempo, chasing my orgasm now, and he grips the back of my neck hard and pulls my mouth down to his. He kisses me like he's trying to devour me like he wants to fuse us. Then his hands slide down my back to grip my hips and suddenly I'm no longer in control of what's happening between us at all. He's doing everything, moving my body on top of him. I surrender to it completely, giving myself over.

He slams into me hard and I fall apart, shaking and screaming his name into the roar of the wind, and at last, all my worries are forgotten.

As the last echoes of my cries fade into the night, I find myself wrapped in the comforting warmth of his arms. He pulls me close, holding me tightly against his chest as the wind continues its dance around us.

My breath comes in gentle waves, matching the steady rhythm of his own, and the waves at the end of the path. I rest my head against his shoulder, finding solace in the safety of his embrace. His hands gently stroke my back, calming my racing heart as we bask in the aftermath of our passion.

The world around us seems to fade, leaving only the two of us entwined in this intimate moment of shared release. There is a deep sense of contentment, a quiet gratitude for how he makes everything else slip away.

Chapter 8
Christos

Pam dresses slowly and shyly, her back to me as she pulls her clothes back on. It's a little silly, given the situation, but I find it a bit sweet at the same time. I don't begrudge her this shyness. If anything, it only makes me feel more drawn to her.

But I don't share that feeling, so I'm still facing her when I stand up and start doing up my pants. She turns around before I'm finished and blushes furiously. I'm oddly charmed. Not five minutes ago she was begging for my cock, and now this.

"That was something," I say.

"I've never…done anything like that," she says.

"Well, maybe we can change that."

"Do you…?" she asks. "I mean, is this normal for you?"

"Are you asking me if I normally have sex with women on the beach?"

"I guess I am."

"The answer's no. I've never done that before. There is a part of me that wanted to, though."

She grins. "Me too."

"Yeah?"

"It's one of those wild fantasies that you never think you'll follow through on, but…yeah. I'm glad we did."

"Me too." I finish doing up my pants. "Listen, would you like to come to my place for a drink?"

"More wine?"

"I was thinking more along the lines of whiskey. If you'd be into that."

She laughs. "That might make a refreshing change of pace. It's been a while since I drank whiskey."

"I've got some good stuff back at the house." I'm already thinking about which bottle to open. I feel like it's got to be something special since she opened a bottle of Matt's special reserve for me.

We walk along the beach. Now and then, she stops to pick up a rock, studying each one closely. She tosses most of them away, but eventually, she tucks one into her pocket, and my curiosity is piqued. "What's with the rock?" I ask her.

"It's not a rock," she says. "It's a fossil." She pulls it back out of her pocket and offers it to me. I take it, frowning. It looks as if it's been tattooed with vaguely hexagonal shapes. I'm not sure what I'm looking at.

"It's a Petoskey stone," she explains. "Have you never seen one before?"

"No, never."

"It's fossilized coral," she explained. "They're all over the beach here—well, not *all* over. But not that hard to find. I've had a collection since I was a kid."

"I've never heard of this," I say, turning it around in my hand so I can examine it from all sides. I can see the shape of the coral now that she mentions it. It's pretty. I wonder if I could find one of these.

"I'm not surprised," Pam says. "Seeing as how you're new to the area."

I look up at her.

She's grinning. "Did you think I didn't know?"

"Well, it hasn't come up."

"Brian told me," she explains. "You know my brother, Brian, right?"

"Sure, I know Brian." I like Brian. I also think of him as someone much younger than I am, so it's a little bit of a gut check to realize that I've been fucking his sister. But also, his sister's insanely hot and a lot of fun. Even now, I'm itching to bury my fingers in all those cascading crimson locks, pull her close to me, and breathe in the scent of her. It's probably inevitable that Matt and Brian will find out what's been going on here at some point, but I'm not going to live in dread of that moment. I'm going to enjoy this while it lasts.

"Brian mentioned that you've only been around for a few months," Pam explains.

"So you were talking to him about me?" I tease her.

"Yeah, I told him that my rude neighbor was hanging out the window yelling at me." She cocks an eyebrow.

I have to laugh. "Touché," I say. "I guess I was. What did he say to that?"

"He said I shouldn't be too quick to judge you. And I guess he was right."

"Well, I'm glad you've revised your opinion," I tell her.

"So how are you liking Michigan so far?"

"I'm a fan," I say. "I knew there were beaches around the Great Lakes, of course, but until I moved here, I had only ever seen the coastline in downtown Chicago. And that's very different. So urban. You stand on the beach and look back at the city."

"Is that where you're from? Chicago?"

"That's where I grew up. My parents came to the US from Greece when I was little, and my father opened a restaurant in Greektown near

Detroit. That's where I learned to appreciate wine in the first place. I was always entranced by how our sommelier described the different varietals. I used to follow him around while he worked."

"Your parents were all right with that?"

"Yeah. They thought it was cute that I took such an interest, as long as I didn't get in the way of things, which I learned quickly not to do." We've reached my house now, and I open the door and stand back to let her in first.

Pam looks around wonderingly as she steps inside. "This place is *so* nice," she says.

I take in my home, trying to see it through fresh eyes. It's certainly not the biggest or the most luxurious house I've ever owned. I bought it for its location. It *is* nice, though. I can acknowledge that much.

"Let's go to the upstairs den," I suggest.

She boggles slightly at that. "The *upstairs* den? Meaning you also have a downstairs den?"

"The upstairs one is private, usually. And the view of the lake is amazing. The downstairs one is for socializing." Not that I've done any socializing since I moved here, but if I was *going* to have guests over, I always figured the downstairs den would be a place I'd entertain them.

I might have to rethink that, of course, given that I'm rushing Pam right upstairs—but I don't think that reflects how I'd treat a more typical guest. There's nothing typical about Pam, and I am not embarrassed to admit that I'm trying to impress her here.

We go up the stairs and down the hall. The upstairs den has sliding French doors, which I keep open because they're so heavy and I don't have any real reason to close them. I usher her inside and indicate a chair for her to sit down. She takes a seat and looks around expectantly. "You've got whiskey in here?"

"Over here." I take it two highball glasses I keep on my bookshelf down. "I've been saving this bottle for a special occasion."

"Oh, and what special occasion is this?"

"We're celebrating the night I got you to strip naked on a public beach using nothing more than the power of persuasion," I tell her, handing her a glass.

Pam grins at me. "That's selling yourself short," she informs me. "You could have persuaded me all day long and it wouldn't have made any difference if I hadn't known there was a good fuck in it for me."

"Fair enough." I raise my glass. "We're celebrating a good fuck, then."

"I'll drink to that," she says. "So, what brings you up north anyway?"

Ah. Now we're getting into a thorny area. I don't think I can tell her the real reason I moved here—not knowing that I'm locked in a property bidding war with her family. I don't want her to know about that, because if she does, she'll tell Matt. I'm not sure if there's anything Matt could do about it, but it might make things hostile between us. Eventually, of course, he'll be told that I'm the one bidding against him. He'll know when I own the land if nothing else. But in this case, I think it might be easier to ask for forgiveness than permission. That's what I'm hoping for, at any rate.

"I wanted to live near a vineyard," I tell her because that's the closest thing I can say to the truth. "Since I've always loved wine so much, I thought it made sense to live close to it."

She nods. "Do you own property anywhere else?"

"What do you mean? What makes you ask that?"

She shrugs. "Brian says you're not always here," she explains. "He says sometimes you go away and he and Dad don't know where you've gone or when you'll be back. It sounded to me like maybe you split your time between two different homes."

Great. Here's another thing I can't talk to her about. This is turning out to be a much more complicated night than I'd expected.

Retiring from active Navy SEALs when I did was the right move for me. I've never questioned that. But my privatized rapid response rescue organization gives meaning to my life. The trouble is, it's not the type of thing you can tell people. For safety reasons, we have to maintain a degree of secrecy. I can't brag to women I'm sleeping with about how I run a tight-knit group of ex-military men and women, and that sometimes our missions take me away from here—out of the country.

She doesn't need to know that, at least for now.

"I travel a lot," I tell her because it's the truth and I don't know what else to say. She smiles and the conversation moves on, and for now, at least, I've dodged a bullet.

I wonder how long it will be until this comes up again. I won't be able to keep this secret forever.

Chapter 9
Pamela

The fact that I've convinced Christos to come into town with me today feels like nothing short of a miracle. I can tell he's not the window-shopping type, and the fact that I feel like walking up and down the familiar streets of Fishtown and checking out the boats in the harbor doesn't strike me as a compelling enough reason for him to leave his house. I did not think he would join me today when I asked him to. It was more of a formality that I made the request at all.

And yet here he is, walking alongside me in the late morning sun. I'm half-tempted to reach out and take his hand as we walk past the docks. It's a silly impulse, of course. The two of us are not dating. We don't have a relationship that would include walking hand in hand by a picturesque harbor. He'd probably think I was crazy if I tried it. Hell, it probably would be crazy to try it.

But there's still something appealing about the notion. His hand in mine, leaning against his shoulder, letting everyone in town see my claim on this man. Because I *do* have a claim here. It might not be a romantic one. It might be purely physical—but no, that's not accurate. It is *something* more than physical. I know it is because he's here with me now, because we spend time together with our clothes on from time to time. He likes me as a person. I like *him* that way too. The two of us—we're friends, I suppose.

Friends who fuck, but friends nonetheless.

But friends don't hold each other's hands on downtown strolls, so I distance myself from him a little and stuff my hands in my pockets instead. "How do you like the view?" I ask him.

"Very pretty." I think he's saying that to be polite, more than anything else, but I don't mind because it's the truth.

"This was always one of my favorite places," I tell him. "When Brian was old enough to be responsible for the two of us for a day, we started coming down here. We'd pack lunches and sit on the edge of the pier, watch the boats leave and come back. We used to talk about how we'd get a boat of our own someday, when we were both grown up."

He nods like that's something to take seriously. "Did you ever do it?"

"Get a boat? No, I haven't got a boat." I laugh. "I don't have that much of a disposable income. Maybe I could save up and buy one, but the docking fees and the upkeep—it wouldn't be worth it. Besides, I'm too busy with the vineyard. I'd never have time to take it out of the harbor. It would sit around here rusting, and that would be a tragic waste."

"Maybe I should get a boat," he muses.

"Do you know how to sail?"

"Sure."

"You're kidding. You learned that —-where?"

"Chicago, that is on Lake Michigan too," he reminds me.

"That's true. I don't think of it as an especially aquatic place."

"Yeah, it's not. I've always liked being on the water, so I went out of my way to learn, that's all."

I nod. "Well, if you get a boat, you'll have to take me out on it," I tell him.

"Yeah? Would you like that?"

"Boats are sexy." I'm flirting pretty shamelessly here, but so is he. And anyway, it's fun to flirt with him. It's fun to banter and wonder where things will go next. I have a pretty good idea of where I want things to go. Maybe we leave Fishtown and head back to my place—or his place—and have sex at one of our homes, for once. I can't believe we haven't done that yet. This is the most adventurous relationship I've ever been in. If it's fair to call it a relationship. Jean-Luc was never up for anything exciting sexually.

I turn away from the water. "Do you want to get going?" I ask him. "I need to hit the fabric store before it closes."

"What do you need from the fabric store?"

"Fabric."

"Ha-ha," he deadpans.

I grin. "I'm going to make a new dress," I tell him. "Nothing fancy."

"I didn't know you made clothes."

"I don't. This will be my first time. I've always wanted to try, but I didn't dare while I was in France. Everyone's so fashionable there."

"But not here, huh?"

"It's not anything like the same thing. Here I could put together a basic sundress, and if it is simple, it would come off as charming and quaint."

"You may be right about that. I hope you'll show it to me when it's finished."

"You still haven't promised to take me out on your hypothetical boat," I tease him.

He laughs. "You show me the sundress and I'll take you out on the boat."

"Deal. Hey, do you think—" I stop mid-sentence when his face changes from his sexy smirk. "What is it? Why do you look like that?"

He puts a hand on my shoulder and turns me in place, and momentarily I am struck dumb.

It's Dad. Dad is standing at the far end of the pier. And he's staring at the two of us like he doesn't know what to make of what he's seeing.

For a moment, neither of us moves or says anything, but Christos rallies. "It's okay," he murmurs to me. "Let's go over and talk to him."

"He isn't going to like this," I say softly.

"We aren't doing anything wrong. What's not to like? We came into town together and we're looking at boats."

"That's one hell of a spin job." I can think of one thing about our situation that my father would dislike if he knew. Christos might be confident that what's about to happen to go smoothly, but I know better. I know my father better. He's impossible to fool and quick to judge. He will figure out that there is something between me and Christos, and he won't like it.

But he's seen us. Now there's nothing to do but face him and talk it out. I want to reach for Christos' hand that much more, to reassure myself that I have someone on my side in all this, but to do that in front of Dad would be leagues worse than doing it on the streets of Fishtown where people might be watching, but none of them truly mattered.

I square my shoulders. I can handle this.

Christos and I walk over to Dad. "Hey, Matt," Christos says.

"Chris," Dad returns, and I can't decode his tone of voice. I know my father well. I can usually tell if he's upset, but his face is a mask right now.

"Nice to see you," Christos offers.

Dad doesn't return that sentiment. He waves a hand at the two of us. "You two run into each other here?"

Ooh, I'd love to tell him yes. It would cut all the tension because he can't object to us bumping into one another, or to the fact that we would stop to chat.

But also, I don't want to lie. Not because my father is owed the truth here—I respect him, but I don't need to tell him about my love life. It's more that I want to be honest about Christos. I don't want to try to hide him. That would feel wrong. I mean, I'm certainly not going to tell Dad that we fucked on the beach, but I do want to be honest about the fact that we've been spending time together. I can't see why I should have to lie about that.

I clear my throat and say, "We came together."

Christos coughs. I hear the double meaning in my words and fight not to blush.

"You came into town together?" Dad asks, frowning, and I can see him trying to put the pieces together.

"We are neighbors," I remind him.

"I don't go shopping with my neighbors. I don't stand on the pier and look at the water with them."

"Pam has been showing me around town," Christos offers.

"You've lived here for months. I know you've seen the town by now."

This is getting ridiculous. "We've been spending time together, Dad," I say. "We get along pretty well. We're friends."

Dad cocks an eyebrow. "Friends, huh?"

"I can't make friends?"

"*He* can't," Dad says. "I've never seen you make a friend, Chris. You come to the vineyard to work and barely talk to anyone who isn't me. You vanish for weeks without telling anyone where you're going. Now you're hanging around my daughter? What's your angle?"

"Dad!" I can't believe him.

"I don't have an angle," Christos says. "I enjoy her company. Can you blame me for that?"

"Maybe not, but I can blame you for interfering in her life. Pam has an incredibly promising future, Chris. She doesn't need to be jerked around and distracted by someone who can't commit to anything."

"Stop it, Dad," I snap. "I'm not asking him to *commit* to anything. We're hanging out in Fishtown for the day. You're being ridiculous."

"You and I are going to talk about this later," he informs me.

I shrug. "That's fine. We can talk all you want." He still thinks I'm seventeen years old and that the threat of a talking-to carries some weight to intimidate me into doing what he wants. If he believes that, he's dreaming.

Dad glares at Christos, then turns around and walks off, leaving both of us in stunned disbelief.

Chapter 10
Christos

I'm still irritated about the encounter with Matt when we get back home. We pause on the path between our houses—the first place I saw her—and the silence is incredibly awkward. I have no idea what to say to her, and I'm unsure how to respond to what her father just said.

Pam looks up at me. "I'm so sorry about Dad," she says. "I don't know what the hell got into him."

"I guess he doesn't like me dating his only daughter."

"But we're not *dating*." She hesitates. "Are we?"

"I don't know. It probably looks to him like we are." I shrug. "I wouldn't split hairs with him on that point. Functionally, there's not much of a difference between hanging out all the time and having sex versus dating. I don't think it would make him feel better if we tried to argue that we're not putting a label on it. I don't think that's his issue."

She chuckles, and I'm relieved to have gotten some mirth out of her, at least. "You've got that right," she says. "Imagine telling him that we're only fucking and it's not that serious." She lowers her voice comically. *"Oh, all right, that's no problem then."*

I laugh too. I'm glad it's funny. It makes it easier to take the whole thing in stride. "What do you want to do about it?" I ask her.

She shrugs. "You're the one who's got to decide," she says. "I don't need my father's approval on my social life. He'll always love me, even if he doesn't like what I'm doing. But you might put your relationship with him on the line if we keep this up." She meets my eyes. "If you want to stop, we can stop. If you want to prioritize your friendship with him, I'll back off."

"I don't want you to back off." I would actively hate that.

"What do you want, then?" she asks.

And the answer to that question is as simple as it could be.

I pull her into my arms and kiss her hard, and immediately the swell of passion between the two of us drives out the memory of our encounter with Matt. I can't even think about Matt. It's impossible to care about how he would feel if he came along and saw me here with Pamela. All that matters now is how I feel, and how she feels.

I know she's digging it because she's kissing me back as fiercely as I'm kissing her. The tension is climbing. She wraps her arms around my neck and pulls me close, and arousal pours through me.

I push her back, holding her at arm's length. Her eyes search mine, curious and anxious.

"Inside," I explain.

She nods and grabs my hand, pulling me along the path and through the gate that leads to Rose Crawford's place. I've had my eye on this house for months, but I've never been inside, and as she pulls me through the door, there's a part of me that wants to stop and look around, see what it's like.

But not a big enough part to stop what we're doing for a tour of the place. I have other interests at the moment—that won't be shifted aside for anything as trifling as real estate.

The moment the door is closed behind us, I lift Pam in my arms and she wraps her legs around my waist. I pull her shirt over her head and toss it aside, then pull down the straps of her bra and tug the band low so it's dangling around her waist. She starts to unbutton my shirt too, and I want to let her, but also her perfect breasts are right in my face now, and no human man could resist. I grip them, relishing how firm but soft they are. Pamela hums happily and leans back to give me better access, and I take advantage by leaning down and taking her nipple into my mouth. I flick my tongue against it, then bite down gently and shake my head a little, and I feel a shiver go through her body.

"Bedroom," she says hoarsely.

I don't know where the bedroom is, but I am beyond willing to figure it out. I start down the only hallway I see. There are a few doors, and she reaches out and catches the frame of one of them with her hand, towing us toward and through it. Sure enough, there's the bed. I don't know when I've been so happy to see a piece of furniture.

I sit down on the edge of the bed with her straddling my lap and work my hands down the back of her shorts to grip her ass, dragging her against me. I can feel the heat of her through our clothes. I'm so hungry for her that I feel like I might lose my mind, and the knowledge that this has to stay secret, now that we're doing this in defiance of Matt, makes it that much hotter somehow. Her father disapproves, and she's choosing to be with me anyway. I've got to make it worth her while.

I lay back on the bed so that she's lying on top of me, which gives me the leverage I need to get her shorts off. I work a hand between our bodies and press a finger into her, then a second one. Pam rocks on my hand, throwing her head back, her long hair hanging so far down that I can feel it brushing against my thighs.

Her response to my touch is immediate, her body arching against me as she lets out a low moan. Her eyes are closed, and I can see the pleasure playing across her features, every movement drawing me further into the intoxicating dance of our connection. My free hand finds the curve of her back, pulling her closer, her softness melding perfectly against me.

She shifts her hips, pressing into my touch with increasing urgency, each motion sending a pulse of heat through me. Her lips part as she breathes heavily, and I take the opportunity to capture her mouth in a searing kiss. The taste of her is as heady as the moment, and our kiss deepens as she grinds against me, the friction intensifying the desire burning between us. With each shared breath and touch, we move together, building a rhythm that is both sensual and electric, a prelude to the passion that is just beginning.

The way she moves against me sends a shockwave of desire through my body. Her skin is warm and smooth, and the sound of her quickening breaths in my ear drives me to the edge. As her hips roll against me, the heat between us builds, each brush of her body against mine fanning the flames. Her fingers grip my shoulders, drawing me in closer, and the urgency in her touch echoes my own.

I can't wait anymore. I need her.

I roll us over and kick off my pants. Gripping her ankles, I spread her legs and push her knees up nearly to her ears. She looks at me, hungry and longing and biting her lip. She is the sexiest thing I've ever seen, and I want to make her mine.

I thrust into her and she cries out. I let out a groan myself. She feels *so* good, hot and wet and tight, and for a moment I don't move at all, letting myself revel in the feeling of being joined with her. But I can't maintain that for long. The need is rising in me and I have to fuck her.

Her head thrashes as I push into her, her hips bucking off the bed to meet me. I sink into the rhythm of it, enjoying the sound of our skin slapping together. It's quick and hard and dirty, exactly what the tension of the day calls for.

Her legs start to shake. She's close.

"Come for me," I breathe.

And that's all it takes. She lets out a cry of ecstasy and clamps down around me. Her toes flex and her teeth grit together so hard I'd almost worry about her, but my pleasure is mounting and it's too hard to think about anything except the fireworks building beneath my skin. I fuck her hard through her orgasm, slamming deep into her, and as she starts to come down, I reach my breaking point. An animalistic growl tears through me and I give her three more good hard thrusts as I come, and then I pull out and fall to one side, pulling her with me to lie on my chest as our bodies start to cool.

Neither of us says anything for a moment. We lie there, letting our breathing return to normal, and I run my fingers slowly up and down her arm, loving the feel of her soft, perfect skin, breathing her in. She's still shivering with aftershocks, and she holds me making me feel like I'm her anchor. It's a powerful feeling.

"We're definitely not letting my father keep us apart from each other," she says after a few moments have passed.

"No way," I agree lazily. I like Matt. I respect Matt. But Matt doesn't tell me what to do, never has, and there is no force alive that will keep me away from Pam. We enjoy this too much to be turned away from—however we want to define this. We'll have to keep it between us, that's all. We'll have to play it cool. It'll be tricky since we live so close to Matt and we both work in the vineyard almost every day. But I believe we can pull it off. She's certainly worth the effort.

I turn to face her and kiss her again, with a sense of smug satisfaction. Matt might not think I'm good enough to be involved with his daughter, but *she* sure thinks I am, and at the end of the day, that's all I care about.

Chapter 11
Pamela

After a few hours, we crawl out of bed. The sun is starting to go down, and I throw open the doors that lead onto the beach. He's shirtless, and I'm dressed in nothing but an oversized t-shirt that fits me like a dress, but this part of the beach belongs to me as long as I'm in this house, so this time we don't have to worry about passersby. Someday this will be my property for real, and I'll be able to build a patio out here that extends toward the water. Until the place is mine, I'm hesitant to put any work into it, because you never know—things might fall through for me here. I might not ever be able to call it my own. I believe I will. I have faith. But until that day comes...I'll wait.

Christos wanders down the beach, stopping after a few yards. "Is this a fire pit?" he calls back to me.

I come up alongside him. He's looking at a hole in the sand. I'd noticed it before, but I never gave it too much thought—I haven't had the chance to spend too much time on this part of the beach.

"Maybe," I say. "Do you think?"

"It *could* be a fire pit," he says. "Do you have any wood?"

"There's a pile of wood on the side of the cottage." I point toward it. "I never thought about it, but it's possible someone collected it at some point to have fires here."

"It's not damp?"

"No, it's under the overhang of a tree, so it's stayed pretty dry."

"Want to give it a try?"

I grin. "Sure." I haven't had a beach bonfire in years. My friends and I used to do it as teenagers, but gradually life became a distraction and we stopped. Right now, it sounds like a fun way to relax and enjoy the evening with Christos, and I'm up for the idea. "Think we'll be able to see the Northern Lights tonight?"

"Probably not," he says, laughing.

"Hey, sometimes you can see them from here. I have before."

"I won't rule it out." He smiles at me. "At the very least, we'll be able to see some good stars. I'm pretty good at spotting constellations."

"I'm sure I'm better," I say.

"You're on."

We wander down to the pile of driftwood and load up our arms with as much as we can carry in our arms. When we get back to the pit, we break off smaller pieces of tinder to start our fire. I can tell Christos has done this before, probably as many times as I have, because he doesn't seem to need any instruction. We work in tandem easily, without speaking. When the tinder is laid in the pit, he pulls a lighter out of his pocket and flicks it once, and the flames begin to dance.

I find small pieces of wood to add, one by one, letting the fire catch and build. Eventually, it reaches the point where I'm comfortable adding a larger log, and once that's burning steadily, Christos and I sit back. He wraps an arm around my shoulders and I lean against his chest.

"The Big Dipper," I tell him, pointing it out.

He chuckles. "That's the best you've got? The big dipper?"

"Hey, the Big Dipper is cool."

"It's also the easiest constellation in the world to spot."

"Fine. Sagittarius." I point.

"That's more like it. Ursa Major."

We go on that way for a while, trading the names of star patterns. He is good—he's able to keep up with me, which no one else in my life has ever been able to do, apart from my brother Brian. Eventually, we fall silent, listening to the sounds of the waves on the shore.

I can't remember the last time I felt this comfortable and at ease in a man's arms. It was never like this with Jean-Luc, that's for sure. I was always a little anxious with him, always worried that I would lose his interest. I let myself believe that because I cared for him, and the possibility of losing him had the power to hurt me. Now, I don't think that's the reason, I know I would hate to lose what Christos and I have, but he doesn't make me fear it. I never sense disinterest from him.

Still, thoughts of what my father said are on my mind—not because I have any intention of listening to my father's warnings, but because they've left me curious. I turn a bit in Christos' arms to look up at him. "Where do you go when you aren't here?" I ask him.

"This again?"

"You told me you travel a lot, but where? I'm interested. I want to know."

He sighs. "It's not something I usually share."

"Is it a secret?"

"It's a little bit secret."

"Well, I'm not *less* interested now. You can tell me," I urge him. "I'm not going to tell anyone your secrets, Christos. It's you and me."

He looks at me like that truly means something. I think it does. He might value what's between us as much as I'm starting to. And for the first time, I wonder whether—although we haven't defined it—this might be a relationship after all.

"Okay," he says. "But you won't tell anyone, right? Not even your father."

"No one."

"Ever."

"Ever."

"I'm a semi-retired Navy SEAL," he says.

"That's the secret?"

"No, that part isn't a secret. People know about that. But after I retired, I developed a piece of technology used in foreign ops surveillance. It's complicated—I won't try to explain how it works. Most of it's classified, so I couldn't tell you even if it was easy to understand. I can say this, we get a lot of information about what's happening in foreign countries because of this technology. It's very powerful.

"Wow," I murmur. "And here I thought you were nothing but the grouchy crank next door with a passion for wine."

He chuckles and I enjoy the sensation of his body moving against mine. "A little more than that," he says.

"So that's where you go when you're not here? To...what, to work on your tech thing or something?" I'm unclear why you leave town, especially without telling anyone where he's going.

"No, that's only part of it," he says. "The rest is a little more complicated."

"Tell me," I urge.

He nods slowly. "All right," he agrees. "I run an organization of retired military folks."

"What organization? What does it do?"

"A rapid response team. Our job is to be boots on the ground in a hurry when the US military isn't able to mobilize as quickly. They have to wait for orders from up the ladder, but because we're a private organization, we can move fast. We work in communication with the military—they tell us when there's a need somewhere, and we go in and do what needs to be done."

"I'm not sure I understand," I admit. "It sounds like you're describing a branch of the military."

"No, it's more like a special forces unit—but an independent one, not a branch of the US government."

"What kinds of things do you do?"

"Oh—for example, there was an incident last year where a couple of American exchange students got themselves into a hostage situation in Eastern Europe."

"I think I saw that on the news," I recall.

"You probably did. What you wouldn't have seen was, while senators debated how involved our military could be in that affair, my team was able to go in and extract them, bring them safely home."

"That sounds so dangerous!" I can't believe what I'm hearing. "You could have been killed. How could you do something so dangerous?"

"There's always that risk in a military operation," he says. "You recognize some things are bigger than your own life if you're going into the service."

"But you're not in the service. You're retired. You shouldn't be doing these things, should you?" I can't pretend it doesn't cause me anxiety to think of him in that situation. I hate the idea of Christos running into danger like that—and the fact that I'm reacting as strongly as I am to it makes me realize, more powerfully than anything else has so far, that I've become attached to him. I can't take the thought of anything happening to him.

He chuckles lightly. "It isn't anywhere near as dangerous as you're thinking," he assures me. "I know there are some intimidating phrases in what I said, but we do everything safely. You don't need to worry about it."

I want to keep pressing that, but —what else can I do? I nod slowly. "Promise me you aren't doing anything too insane."

"We only go where we're needed." He picks up a piece of wood and tosses it on the fire, and we both watch as it's slowly consumed by the flames. "It isn't like we're some group of daredevils always flinging ourselves into danger. We go when we have to, and we take every possible precaution. I take the safety of my team extremely seriously."

I nod. "It *is* pretty impressive," I tell him. "I have to admit, I don't think I could do something like that. I mean, even if I did have the training for it. Once I was retired, I think I would want to relax."

"Relaxing all the time gets boring," he says. "And if you don't put your skills to work, you lose them. Besides—I don't know if it's something everyone can understand, the way it feels to have someone's life in your hands and to know that they're going to survive because of you. To know that you're bringing such good to the world in such a powerful way—there's nothing like that feeling, and that's what my team can do. I don't think I'd feel right if we *didn't* do the things we do, knowing that we're capable of them."

I'm quiet for a few moments, taking that in. I've never been so filled with admiration for Christos as I am right now. Everything I've thought about him so far pales in comparison to this. He's an extraordinary man, and whatever this thing is between us, I'm proud I can say I'm a part of it. I don't know if it's right to think of myself as belonging to him, but it does feel that way, to an extent, and it's a good feeling.

"Can you tell me?" I ask him at length. "I mean when you're going to be going away? So I'm not taken off guard by it? And so I don't have to panic every time I can't get in touch with you?"

"I can't promise that," he says. "There's usually not a lot of notice. We have to leave quickly when something comes up, so there isn't time to make phone calls. And for the sake of security, we can't let people know where we're going. But I can promise you that I'll always take your calls, or at the very least, call you back quickly. That way you won't have to worry. I know it puts people in a hard position when they have to wonder about where members of the team are—although, it's never happened to me before."

"What do you mean?"

He shrugs. I feel the rise and fall of his shoulders. "There's never been anyone who would care that much about my absence," he explains. "Only your father and brother would notice it, and I think they decided I was unreliable for no good reason. They weren't angry about it since I was unpaid labor anyway, and they like me—well, they did." His arms tighten around me. "Who knows what they'll think of me now."

"Dad will get over his crap," I assure Christos. "Don't worry. He can't be angry at me for having a life."

Christos doesn't respond, but he doesn't have to. I know what he's thinking because I'm thinking it too.

I'm not the one my father would be angry at.

Chapter 12
Pamela

"I love what you've done with the place, Pam," Rose Crawford says enthusiastically as I remove the tea kettle from the stove and pour hot water into both of our mugs.

I chuckle. "I didn't do anything," I point out. "I moved my furniture in. That's about it."

"But it livens everything up," Rose says happily. "It's so nice to see this place look lived-in again. You wouldn't believe how much it means to me."

She's right, I wouldn't. I like Rose a lot—she's an incredibly sweet woman, in her mid-seventies, and always in a good mood. She's great company. I've known her since I was a little kid—in a town this size you know everyone. She was one of Mom's best friends, and she often spent time with the family swimming, searching for rocks, and long nights of stargazing around the firepit. Her oldest son, Brad, was my first crush, and he and I used to stay out late and make out under the stars. He never came home after college—I hear he's doing something in Silicon Valley now. It's always so bizarre to me when someone leaves. I never could.

Rose and I don't spend much time together nowadays, since Mom's gone. I've seen her at the downtown diner I know is her favorite and I've run into her at the grocery store. But I wouldn't say we were close until the past month or two—since I moved back here and into this house. Odd that I should count her as a friend when she won't sell the place to me—but that's Rose in a nutshell. You can't stay angry at her. At least, I can't.

Besides, I'll get her to sell me the place. It will take a little bit of time, that's all. I'll wear her down eventually.

I hand her her mug of tea and join her at the table. "How have things been going for you?" I ask her.

She sips the tea and waves a hand in my direction. "I'm fine," she says. "But enough about me—I want to hear more about you. You're the one with an interesting life. All my most exciting stories are behind me, but yours are only beginning. Tell me what's been happening in your world. Every time I see you, I think about that freckle-faced little girl I used to see running around on the beach."

I smile. "That feels like a long time ago."

"I know you were off in Paris. You were in school there, I think?"

"That's right," I tell her. "I've been studying to become a sommelier for the vineyard. I was able to finish my mastery certification—level 4."

"I don't know anything about it," Rose says with a laugh. "Is level 4 good?"

I don't like to brag, but she's asking, and I *am* proud of my accomplishments. "It's very good," I say. "Not very many people pass the exams required for that certification. I want to go for level 5 eventually, but it's a big dream. I'll need to put more time into racking up the experience to make that a reality."

"I'm sure you can do it," she says confidently. "I know you can do anything you put your mind to. Your mother would have said the same thing."

I smile. I appreciate her confidence in me, even though it will be a lot more complicated than simply doing it because I set my mind to it. Even my current mastery level is pretty rare and hard to attain. Most people fail the exams I had to pass to get to where I am. It's one of the reasons I was so excited about the prospect of opening a restaurant on the property and giving myself the chance to show off my new sommelier skills to their fullest extent. I have visions of working with a top chef, putting together exquisite pairings, and planning the intricacies of a menu so that I can recommend the perfect wine to complement each dish. I've studied hard and earned my stripes, and I know I'll be great at that.

At least, I *would* be if I got the chance.

I try to put that thought out of my mind. I don't want to spend today being miserable about things that aren't going to happen. It sucks spending all my time thinking about what might have been. Instead, I go to the counter beside the refrigerator, to the two bottles of wine I was opening when Rose dropped by. "Do you want to try something?" I ask her. "I've been looking for another set of taste buds on this."

"One of your father's wines?"

"Not exactly." I measure out a little bit from each bottle, eyeing the glass carefully. I haven't tried this combination yet, but I've been thinking about it since before I boarded the plane home from France. "These are Dad's wines, but I'm trying something new with them here." I hand her the glass. "See what you think of that."

She swirls it, blending the flavors, and then takes a sip. I know it's not the perfect experiment, since she's been drinking tea, but it wouldn't have been perfect anyway. What I want to do in the long term is develop a new grape varietal unique to our vineyard, our own pink Riesling. I haven't had time to cultivate that, so what I've got today is an experiment to see if I can get close to the taste I eventually want to create. I'm using Dad's Riesling and a little bit of the Pinot Noir today, and I know it's perfect, but the color looks good and maybe the flavor will be something close to what I want.

Rose sips it tentatively, allowing herself time to experience the flavor. She's a good wine drinker, as most locals are. Nothing's more annoying to me than people who throw it back like they're taking a tequila shot. Thankfully, I didn't have to deal with that much in France, and it's not that common here at MacLaine either, but this *is* a touristy town, and we do get people on occasion who are taking their first foray into experiences with fine wines. I usually love them, because they're so often eager to learn and excited to try things, but occasionally, you get someone who seems to feel like the point of wine is to get drunk.

Rose isn't like that. She grew up around wineries and tasting rooms, the way I did. I'm sure she's almost as familiar with all of this as the members of my own family. Everyone local knows all about wine.

Rose smiles at me. "This is good," she says. "Very good."

"I'm so glad you like it. I'm hoping to start producing something like it eventually." I don't go into the details. I don't want to get into the story of what's holding me back.

"When are you planning to settle down and start a family?" Rose eyes me shrewdly.

I have to laugh. "No plans on that front. Not yet."

"I saw you downtown the other day with that nice young man who lives next door," she says. "You two looked pretty cozy to me."

It's so disorienting to hear her call Christos *that nice young man*. I wouldn't have used either of those descriptors. He can be kind when he wants to, but *nice* isn't the word that comes to mind. And as for *young*—well, he's nearly twenty years older than I am.

"Please keep that to yourself," I tell Rose. I don't know whether it's okay to tell her the truth or not—we've only discussed keeping it secret from my family—and I'm not sure I'd want to talk about it with her anyway.

"Well," Rose murmurs, swirling her wine knowingly, "whatever you are, I'd be mindful, honey. A good man like that doesn't stay on the market very long. Or don't you want to settle down and start a family someday? I'm sure your mother would have liked that."

She's looking at me like this is a question of dire importance. And though it makes me uncomfortable, I do feel compelled at the very least to give her an answer.

So I nod. "I'd like that," I say. "Some of my best memories are of my childhood here. I'd like to raise a family of my own. Maybe someday that will happen. But right now, I need to keep my focus on my work. Until I've achieved my goals, I can't take my foot off the gas—not for anything. Not even for love."

Chapter 13
Christos

"You'll never guess who stopped by my place today," I tell Pam as she takes the lasagna out of the oven. "That smells amazing, by the way. Thanks for cooking."

"Try not to judge me too harshly," she says with a laugh. "My skills are miles outside the kitchen. But who stopped by?"

"Rose Crawford," I say. "You know her, right? She owns this house."

Is it my mistake, or does Pam startle slightly at the sound of the name? "I didn't know you knew Rose," she says carefully. "How did that come to pass when you've lived here such a short time? I know her because I've known her all my life, but it's a surprise to me that *you* do."

"It's a bit of a funny story," I tell her.

"I've got a sense of humor." She grins playfully at me. It's no mistake—she definitely has a sense of humor. It's one of the things I enjoy most about her, though by no means the only thing.

"Let's get that lasagna going first," I suggest. "I'm starving, and I bet you are too after picking grapes all day."

She laughs. "You're not wrong. It was rough out there today."

"We got a lot done though. I'm sure your father is happy."

"For now he is."

I know what she's saying. Obviously, Matt would be a whole lot less happy if he knew that Pam and I were still seeing each other. Not that either of us has plans to tell him that any time soon. But it would make life a lot easier if we could. It's tough walking around the vineyard with her there, working right next to her, watching her red curls start to spill down out of her ponytail, the wind occasionally catching the scent of her and carrying it to me—it's hard to work under those conditions and know I can't grab her and kiss her, or even do more than make pleasant small talk. I can't even ignore her, because *that* would be weird and would definitely alert Matt to the fact that things were different than what they appeared between the two of us. It's maddening.

There is a huge part of me that wants to say fuck it, let Matt get mad. I'd probably do it if Pam would let me. I'm the one Matt wouldn't forgive—he's not going to stay mad at his daughter—and I'm willing to take that on. She won't let me do it, though. She's too kindhearted for her own good sometimes.

She puts a slice of lasagna on a plate in front of me. "Careful," she says. "It's pretty hot."

"Oh, I can handle it." There's no way I'm waiting to eat my lasagna. I fork up a big bite, shove it in my mouth, and immediately regret it. She was right. This is way too hot to eat right away. Still, I've got to try to look cool, so I force myself to chew it up and swallow.

She's laughing at me, seeing right through my façade. "I told you to wait!" she says. "You didn't even get to experience the taste of it, bolting it down like that! And I specifically picked that cabernet to go with it. Snack on peanuts if you're so hungry you can't wait a few minutes for it to cool." She pushes a bowl toward me.

"I can wait," I say. I don't want to ruin my appetite. She's clearly gone all out on this meal. I pick up my wine glass. "This isn't from your dad's vineyard, is it? I don't recognize the label."

"It isn't, no. Dad's cabernet didn't have quite the flavor I was looking for here, so I went into town and picked something up. This is a particular favorite of mine, though. I drank a lot of it while I was in France. I'm glad you can get it around here."

I nod. I don't know how she is at lasagna, but I am one hundred percent confident in Pamela's ability to choose a good wine. I haven't told her this, and I don't think I will, but I looked up the institution where she studied on my computer a few nights ago. It's prestigious. I can only imagine how thrilled Matt must be to be able to add that level of expertise to his vineyard. Now he doesn't even have to hire a great sommelier—he's got one right in the family, ready to go.

"So," she says, sitting down opposite me at the table. "How is it you know Rose?"

"Oh," I say grinning. "It's a bit of a funny story. I was thinking about buying this house."

Her face freezes for a moment, grin and all.

"My house?" she asks after a moment.

"Well, this was before you moved in," I tell her. "I still might do it someday. I don't know. For right now, Rose isn't selling, which is annoying—I was hoping to own the whole stretch of beach along here."

"I guess Rose wanted to rent," Pam says slowly in an icy tone.

"Yeah, I guess she did. And that's okay. I can wait. I'm glad she decided to rent. I wasn't at first, but now, I met you. So until you're ready to move somewhere more permanent, I'm happy to wait it out."

"Right," Pamela agrees. She bites her lip, and I feel something's upsetting her. I'm about to ask when she looks up, her expression clear. "That lasagna's probably cool now if you want to try it," she says.

I do want to try it. But I'm not sure I should be leaving this subject quite yet. She's smiling at me, but there's something not quite right. It's like she's putting on a show of happiness, but she's not truly happy.

But I must be reading into that. I can't see what she would be unhappy about. We've been having a nice time tonight. Maybe I'm stressing her out by talking about a future she doesn't feel ready to talk about. After all, I don't think she has plans for what she's going to do when she moves out of this place.

Unless—is it possible *she* wants to buy this house?

Oh, hell. That can't be it, can it?

Bad enough that I'm in a property war with her father. We could probably get past that, I think—Pam's already shown me that she's willing to side with me over her father when push comes to shove, so I think she'd forgive me there. But her wanting this house—if it's true—that's something else. That's something personal, for her.

Should I back off and let her have it?

For a moment I think maybe I should...but then I change my mind. If that was what this was about, she would tell me. She wouldn't leave me guessing. Not if it was important. If I make a big production about letting her have the house she's already living in, I'll come off cocky and arrogant. If she brings the matter up with me, we'll talk about it, but until she does, I should leave it alone. That seems for the best.

At least we have the lasagna to distract us from the situation. I fork up another bite, this one smaller than the last. I taste it gingerly and see that Pamela was right—it's cool enough now.

And it's delicious. I don't hesitate to tell her so. "This is *amazing*," I say honestly. "I thought you told me you weren't a very good cook!"

She blushes, and the smile on her face looks genuine once more. Whatever was bothering her, I see I've cleared it from her mind for the moment. "This is my grandmother's recipe," she says. "After she died, I spent years perfecting it. It felt like a way to keep her alive."

"You did great," I assure her. "Not that I ever tasted your grandmother's version, of course—but this is delicious, so I'm sure she'd be proud of you for it."

She reaches across the table and takes my hand. "Thanks, Christos," she says quietly. "It means a lot to me to hear you say that."

She gives my hand a quick squeeze and lets go, leaving me confused—but in a good way. I've never had this before. I've never been so involved with a woman that I wanted to say kind things to make her feel better about serious situations. I've certainly never known what those things would be.

And until I met Pamela, that never seemed very important. It didn't seem to matter that I didn't know what to say to someone who was going through hard times. There was no reason anyone would turn to me at a time like that anyway.

But Pamela would. Pamela needs me in a way nobody has before, and it truly means the world to me. For her sake, I'll find the words she needs to hear a million times.

Chapter 14
Pamela

"So what's going on with you and Chris?"

"Nothing's going on," I say in protest.

"Pamela, come on. I left it alone when I saw the two of you in town, but I wasn't born yesterday," Dad says. "Hand me that garbage bag, will you?"

The two of us are in the tasting room, cleaning up cocktail napkins and other rubbish from the day's tasting, which I ran—something I wouldn't have been able to do before my schooling in France. I'm proud of how it went today. I wasn't nervous—I've done this plenty of times, and anyway, wine is one of those topics I could spend hours talking about without breaking a sweat or repeating myself. I think I kept people engaged and everyone had a great time.

Now if only I could figure out how to get them to throw away their garbage.

I hand Dad the bag. "I told you, we were seeing the sights," I tell Dad. "Does it have to be deeper than that?"

"You're forgetting I'm the one who watched you bring boys home and tell me they were *only friends* all through your teen years," he says, an eyebrow cocked. "I've seen this show plenty of times, Pamela. I know every beat of the plot."

"I'm not a teenager *now*," I remind him, but the truth is that he's got me pegged. This was exactly my pattern when I was younger. I'd have a crush on some guy and bring him home so we could make out or fool around a little, and when Dad would inevitably find him at the house, I'd insist we were nothing but friends or study partners. Not that I see what the problem is. Didn't everyone do that in high school?

"Listen," Dad says. "That type of thing might have worked when you were younger, but it's different now."

"Don't you tell me I need to settle down and start a family." Hearing that from a sweet old lady is one thing, but if Dad gives me any guff about needing to start a family, this is going to turn into an argument. He knows I'm not ready for that.

Dad shakes his head. "I wasn't going to say that," he says. "You'll start a family when you want to. Or you won't. That's your business."

"But who I date isn't my business?"

"So you *are* dating him."

I sigh. "I didn't say that."

"You implied it. And I know there's something going on between the two of you, so please don't beat around the bush with me, Pamela. I want to know what the story is."

"Dad, I don't owe you an explanation about this," I remind him. "I'm an adult. You can't tell me who I can and can't see."

"I'm not trying to order you around," Dad says. "But I'm still your father. It's my responsibility to warn you when you're getting too close to something that could have serious consequences for you."

"You make it sound like he's going to murder me in my sleep."

"It's nothing like that. Chris is a nice enough guy. He's not the type of guy a man wants dating his daughter, though."

"Why not? What's the problem? If he's a nice guy…"

"It's what I told you before. He isn't reliable. He takes off for weeks at a time. No one knows where he goes when he's gone."

I don't bother explaining to him that I do happen to know where Christos goes when he's gone. First of all, I don't know if Christos wants people to know about that—there's a reason he was so hesitant even to tell me. It also seems beside the point, if I'm being honest. The point here isn't that Christos has a good excuse for leaving when he does. The point is that he shouldn't have to explain himself to Dad or to anyone else.

And I realize that I'm helping my father put him on trial right now simply by indulging these questions. "It doesn't matter what you say," I tell him. "I've made up my mind about Christos already. I'm enjoying getting to know him. I'm going to keep doing it."

I'm going to have to tell Christos about this conversation, too. That isn't going to be any fun. Hopefully, he won't be upset. We were supposed to keep these things to ourselves, and they're all spilling out already. So much for our secret affair.

"I don't like that," Dad shakes his head.

"Well, it's not up to you," I retort. "But, look, why don't you come out to dinner with me and Christos? This doesn't have to be so awkward. Maybe if you spend some time with the two of us together, you'll feel better. It genuinely is a casual thing. There's no need for any drama about it."

I don't know if I'm telling the truth or not now. Things don't exactly feel casual with Christos. I think about him far too much for that label to be comfortable for the two of us.

But we haven't called it anything else. We haven't named our relationship—hell, we haven't even used the word *relationship*. I can't possibly do that without having settled it with him first. So as far as Dad needs to know, what's going on between me and Christos is nothing but a bit of casual fun.

"I guess we could get dinner," Dad says grudgingly. "That wouldn't be the worst."

So now I have to explain to Christos that not only did I not keep us a secret, he also has to do a meet-the-parents style dinner with Dad and try to make nice. Fucking perfect.

Though it could be worse. I suppose there is hope that this will all somehow result in Dad seeing what I see in Christos. There's a chance we all walk away from this dinner in a better place, and Dad will be able to see his way to accepting me and Christos for whatever the hell it is we are to each other.

It's a slim chance. But a slim chance is still a chance, so I will take it.

"I wanted to talk to you about something else, while I've got you here," I tell Dad.

"Go ahead," he says, and I'm pretty sure that he's as eager for the change of subject as I am.

"What if we could get a chef in to serve appetizers here in the tasting room?"

"*In* the tasting room? Pamela, that'll never work. There are no cooking facilities here, for one thing. I know you're not thinking of hiring a chef and asking him to cook at home and bring the food in with him."

"I wasn't," I say. "I was thinking that we'll have our down payment for the expansion we're not going to be able to buy at our disposal. We could put that money to good use. We could add cooking facilities."

He gives me a skeptical look. "You want to build a kitchen onto the tasting room?"

"I know it's a weird idea."

"We don't have anything like the amount of space we would need to make that practical," Dad says gently. "I get it. You're trying to make the idea of having a chef you can do wine pairings with a little more plausible."

"I got this whole certification, Dad," I say. "I'm not trying to be arrogant here, I promise I'm not. But I'm a master sommelier. You get that. I can't help feeling like I'm wasting that here now that we're not buying the extra land. I keep thinking about all the things I've been dreaming about doing, and how it's not going to happen now… what was the point of all that work and study I did if I'm not going to use the things I learned?"

"I understand," Dad says. "I promise you, I do. And I don't want to lose you to another winery."

"Well, you're not going to lose me," I say. "I'm dedicated to our business, even if I am being underutilized."

He nods. "I appreciate that," he says. "That's what I thought you would say. But I also hate to see your skills wasted, because you're right. You have this great education and all this knowledge—anyone else would kill to have you on their staff. Don't think for a moment that I don't appreciate what I've got."

I know he does, but it's still nice to hear him say it. "Thanks, Dad."

"I can't put a kitchen on the tasting room," he says.

I nod solemnly. I knew he couldn't, if I was being honest with myself. It was a pipe dream.

"But you're right that we should keep thinking," he says. "I think we can come up with a solution here—at the very least, something that will allow you to share your knowledge with people. You were talking about hosting classes for a while, right? You could teach people here in the tasting room. Educate them about how to pair wines well. Teach them to appreciate what they're tasting and the differences between varietals. We could institute six-week classes, maybe, or weekend things."

"We could." I've thought about that myself. Having students from Michigan State and Northwestern Viniculture programs camp at D. H. Day State Park, right at the beach and then bringing them up to the vineyard during the day for an experience picking grapes and learning about different wines. It was part of my original plan for this place, and I would still like to follow through with it.

But it's not nearly enough. It's nothing like what I dreamed of when I got my certification. For someone with my skill level, it's the tip of the iceberg of what I could do, and I know it.

This business means everything to me. I know I'll never leave and seek a better opportunity somewhere else. Everything I've done, all my hard work and study, has been for the hope of making *our* vineyard better. I'm committed to that.

But from where I'm standing, it's hard to see what that will look like.

Chapter 15
Christos

"I can't believe you talked me into this," I murmur under my breath as we walk up to the front door of the restaurant. "We said we were going to keep things a secret from your father."

"I know what we said," Pam says. "He's too smart, Christos. He got it out of me. I don't know what else I could have done, it's not as if I wanted to tell him. But it doesn't matter. He's not in charge of what we do."

I let out a sigh. The thing is, I was fine with Matt finding out about all this. We were keeping it secret for Pamela's sake, not mine. But I never reckoned on having to sit down to dinner with him. That's not going to be any fun at all.

We find Matt at the very back of the restaurant. He's already sitting down, and he doesn't stand up as we approach, even though I would have thought he'd want to give Pamela a hug or something. She doesn't falter. She walks right over, pulls out a chair, and sits down across from him. "Hey, Dad," she says. "Good to see you."

"You two are late," he says, raising an eyebrow. "I've been waiting almost fifteen minutes."

"Well, we said seven thirty," she says, checking her phone. "It's seven thirty-two."

"So you're late."

"Two minutes late. Not fifteen.," she says rolling her eyes. "If you've been waiting fifteen minutes, it's because you got here early."

Matt wrinkles his nose, but he clearly doesn't have any counter to that. Still, I know Pamela hasn't exactly won the point. She's right, but that doesn't negate Matt's objections to anything.

"Well, I'm hungry," Pamela says. "Maybe we should order? Or do you need more time to look at the menu, Dad?"

Damn. I have to admire that. She's put the ball right back in his court, because now he either has to order right away or else admit that he needs more time, that fifteen minutes wasn't long *enough*. His eyebrows pull together as he considers those options, obviously looking for the lesser of two evils. Then he puts a finger up, signaling the waiter.

Point Pamela.

We place our orders and the tension is momentarily dissipated. Matt's not happy to see me, I can tell, but it's hard to express anger at someone when you're hungry and looking forward to a porterhouse steak. Pamela sips her wine and says nothing. I guess she's going to let one of us break the ice.

And I guess it's going to have to be me because Matt sure as shit isn't saying anything. "Thanks for meeting up with us tonight," I say because the most important thing I can do here is try to make nice. "I know you're busy."

"I always have time for Pamela," Matt says pointedly.

I nod—message received. He's here for her, not for me, and that's expected. "I know how important it was to Pamela that you and I find a way to get along," I tell him. "I want that too."

"We've always gotten along fine until you started putting the moves on my daughter," Matt says bluntly. "What the hell did you think you were doing?"

"Dad," Pamela says sharply.

But it's a fair question, and if we're going to make any progress here, we need to be honest with each other. "She's a remarkable woman," I say. "I have a lot of admiration and respect for her."

"Or you wanted to hook up with a woman who's nearly half your age."

"Dad!"

"Be serious with me," Matt says. "Is this a relationship? Or are you fucking around? Are you using my daughter to have a good time until the next time you decide to fuck off out of town without telling anyone? Because I won't have that."

"Dad, that's enough," Pamela cuts him off sharply. "You said you were going to come to dinner and make nice. This isn't nice. And if you want to know what Christos and I are doing together, you might as well ask both of us. It's not like he knows more about it than I do. Unless you think I'm such a fool that I'm genuinely getting taken advantage of here."

"I'm not calling you a fool," Matt says.

"Then please, give me some credit," she says. "I know what I'm doing. I don't need you to take the temperature of how serious my relationship is. I can handle that on my own. All I want from you is an hour of pleasant conversation, all right?"

Matt raises an eyebrow. "You go off to France for a year and come back speaking to me like that?"

She takes a deep breath. "You're right," she says. "I could be more polite. But so could you, Dad. Christos is here having dinner with you because he cares enough about me to want to do that. If he was fucking around, as you so charmingly put it, he wouldn't have bothered, would he?"

She has a point and I can tell Matt knows it. He nods slowly. "All right," he says. "Fine. We'll have dinner. I'll behave myself." He points at me. "But you're on notice."

"Fair enough." I mean, I *am* sleeping with his daughter. I'd probably be pissed off at me too if the roles were reversed. At least, I imagine I would. I don't have a daughter, so I can't realistically fathom how I would feel about it.

We don't speak again until the food arrives, which is probably for the best. Matt will be a little more relaxed and easier to get along with once the edge is taken off his hunger, so I don't try to talk again until he's a few bites deep in his steak. Pamela starts a conversation about the harvest, that has legs, so I nod along and chime in occasionally with one-word responses.

When our meals are half gone that attention fully turns back to me. Matt puts his napkin beside his plate, takes a long drink of beer, and says, "Can we expect you to stick around through the end of the season, Christos?"

"I don't know what the next few months will look like for me," I answer truthfully. I can't predict when and if I'll be called away on a mission. "I'll be here as long as I can. You know the vineyard is important to me."

"I didn't realize you lived in the house next to Pamela's. You own property here?"

"That's right."

"I suppose I always thought you were renting. Buying a place—seems like a big step for someone unsure where he'll be half the time. But maybe committing to things you can't follow through isn't a big deal for you."

"Stop it," Pam groans.

But I hold up a hand. "It's a fair question, Matt," I say. "And I'll tell you my answer. I *do* feel committed to this place. I like it here. I care about the people I've met and love the community and the culture. I want to stay here. I can't be here every waking moment for the rest of my life. I have other things I need to do with my time. But I don't see that as any different from Pam spending a year in France learning to become an expert in her field. Sometimes things take us away from home—but we always come back."

Pam smiles warmly at me and takes my hand. And across the table, I see Matt's expression soften slightly, and I know I've said the right thing.

I take a bite of my steak and nod my approval of it. "This is good."

"It's overcooked," Matt grumbles, but at least now he isn't grumbling at me. I'll take it. Pam rolls her eyes at me when he isn't looking, and I have to hold back a grin.

I think tonight went as well as could be expected. Matt got to yell at me a bit, and I'm hoping that means he'll be ready to let all this go and move on. If we're lucky, he'll get it out of his system. And he *does* seem calmer, so I think there is reason to be optimistic about it.

I pay the tab for us—I think maybe Matt isn't going to let me, but he does—and leave the restaurant feeling uplifted. I didn't want to come here tonight, but now I'm glad I did it. At least I know that I've done all I can, and with luck, Matt will get used to the idea of me dating his daughter. I think we're halfway there already.

Chapter 16
Pamela

"I think it went well, don't you?" I ask Christos.

He smiles at me. "You know him better than I do. How has he been the last couple of days, since we went out to dinner together?"

"His normal self," I say with a laugh. "But I think that's a good thing, you know? He's grumping around, same as he always does. He hasn't tried to talk to me about things between us at all, as a matter of fact. I think he's ready to let it go."

"Well, I hope so," Christos says. "That would be nice. I didn't want him to be angry at us."

"Oh, he's not angry."

"He seemed pretty angry over dinner. But I think you're right. He hasn't called me up to tell me I'm no longer welcome at the vineyard or anything like that. Maybe this is finally going to blow over."

We smile at each other. The mood between us today is so light as to be almost giddy. It feels like the number one problem we've both been stressing about has evaporated into thin air.

Well, maybe the number two problem, for me. There's still the question of my future, and the future of my family's business. I don't know what's in store for me there, but I do know it's not something that's going to be solved by dinner at a steakhouse.

It's also not something I plan on worrying about this morning. Christos has come over to make me breakfast, and I'm hoping breakfast ends with us retiring to bed for some fun, maybe followed by a long nap, and then waking up naked together. I can see the whole day stretching out in front of me, peaceful and idyllic, and I love the way it looks. For once, I'm going to set my troubles aside and focus on the here and now.

"Do you have hot sauce?" Christos asks me.

"You looking to spice things up around here?" I give him my wickedest grin.

"Always."

"It's in the fridge. But the *real* heat is in the bedroom."

"Oh, you don't have to tell me," he says. "Don't worry. I'm gonna want a piece of that after we finish our eggs."

I pour orange juice and grab a bottle of champagne from the fridge. Mimosas sound like a good way to start the day. "Those eggs smell amazing, by the way," I tell him.

"Nothing much. This is how I've made them for years. But they come out nice and fluffy thanks to the milk in them," he says. "I think you'll like them."

He spoons some onto a plate and hands it to me, then makes a plate for himself. I get silverware out and we head to the patio to look at the lake while we eat. We both sit down at the patio table, where Christos begins to dump hot sauce all over his eggs.

I have to laugh at him. "You've got more sauce than eggs on that plate," I point out.

"They're good like this."

"You are going to destroy your taste buds, you know. You're supposed to use hot sauce *moderately*."

"Do I tell you how to eat your eggs?" he asks playfully.

I add a sprinkle of pepper to mine—no hot sauce, even though ordinarily I might have put a little bit. Today I feel like I need to make a point. "You aren't going to be able to taste anything properly for the rest of the day," I inform him. "And you'll have nobody to blame for it but yourself."

He laughs. "I think I'll be all right. Besides, I'm not planning on doing any complicated tasting today. The vineyard isn't even open."

He's right. It's Sunday, and the vineyard isn't opening to the public today. That's why I justify spending the whole day at home and in bed, the way I want to so badly. If people were in the tasting room, I'd feel compelled to be there too. Dad knows everything about wine, but not as much as I do about interacting with people. He can't be counted upon to handle that side of things.

I stare out at the water, contemplating. It's a bit worrying that he needs me so badly and yet can't provide me the opportunity I'm looking for to advance my career. I'll always stay here, I know I will. But I have to be careful. I don't want to feel resentful about it. It's not Dad's fault we aren't able to expand. He's done all he could about it.

"What's up with you?" Christos asks. "You're a million miles away all of a sudden. What's on your mind?"

I shrug. For some reason, I'm not inclined to tell him. Maybe it's because I know he's trying to buy this house. I don't know whether or not he'd back off about that if I told him I wanted to buy it too. I want to believe he would because he already owns a house next door. He doesn't need this one too. It would change my opinion of him if he acknowledged he was keeping me from something I wanted and continued doing it anyway. I don't want to risk having to change my opinion about him. Not now, when things are going so well.

I'm also not sure I'd even want him to give up the house for me. That would be a pretty big deal. I don't know how serious the two of us are, and if he made a gesture like that it would imply that things are heading to a level I'm not remotely sure I'm ready to be at.

And none of this matters anyway, because it's not like it's up to him what happens with the house. It's ultimately up to Rose, and she's made it clear she's not selling to anyone. Why make it a point of conflict?

So it's a lose-lose situation. There's no response that he could give me that would make me happy.

All of which, speaks to why I don't want to tell him about our larger land problems. It would feel like uncorking something I couldn't put a stopper back into. If I start talking to Christos about the properties I'm unable to buy, I'll probably talk to him about all of my dreams going up in smoke. And things might get unpleasant.

"Nothing's on my mind," I tell Christos. "I'm daydreaming. It's been so long since I had a day off that I'm letting my thoughts run away with me."

"What are you daydreaming about," he asks, a broad smile on his face. "Whatever it is, maybe we can make it happen."

"Oh, I'm sure we can," I say, glad to be drawn out of my head. "I've got big plans for you. But after breakfast. It would be a damn shame to let these eggs go to waste. They're delicious."

"Well, now you've got me wishing I had cooked you something different!" he says.

"Live and learn." I fork up a big bite of eggs and make a whole production out of eating it. "I'm going to take my time with this. I don't have anywhere to be today. Do you?"

"Nowhere," he says.

And at that moment, it seems like this will be the best day I've had in a long time. Everything's looking positively golden, and it's hard to imagine what could ruin it.

I shouldn't count my chickens before they hatch. Because as I'm having that thought, Christos' phone rings.

I get an immediate shiver of dread. I shouldn't feel this way about the fact that Christos is answering a phone call, and I'm not sure why I do. Maybe it's making me worry that this is going to mean an interruption to our day somehow. What if it's his ex-military squad calling with a mission for him to go off and complete? What if it means we won't see each other again for a long time? I've known that might happen, but suddenly I'm facing it down and I realize I'm not ready.

Without meaning to do it, I glance at his phone to see who the call is from.

Harrison Cooper.

I feel as if my blood is freezing over. It takes my mind a moment to catch up to what my body seems to know right away.

Harrison Cooper—the owner of the land we've been trying to buy—is calling Christos.

Christos is buying up land in the area. Much more than he needs.

There's an offer far beyond what my family can afford on Cooper's land.

And now Cooper is calling Christos—*no*.

No way. The house I could deal with, but this? This I can't take. This can't be real.

I can't compete with Christos for the plot of land that would make my dreams come true. He can't be the one keeping that land away from me.

Can he?

I put my hand out, covering the phone so he can't take the call, forcing him to look at me instead.

"Why is Harrison Cooper calling you?" I ask him quietly.

Chapter 17
Christos

I'm so full of nervous energy that I feel like I might levitate right off my chair and start hovering.

This moment was bound to come, of course. We will not continue seeing each other without her knowing of my ambition to buy that land. And I can tell by the look on her face now that she already knows what's going on. She will make me say it, but that's not because she doesn't know the answer.

I press the button on the side of my phone to decline the call. That call was important—Harrison was probably calling to offer me the deal—but there'll be no forgiveness for me if I buy the land her father is trying to buy while I'm sitting right in front of her before we've even talked about it, while she's staring at me with that look of shocked disbelief in her eyes. If the two of us have a prayer of getting through this, I need to be honest with her first. I wouldn't even ask her to forgive me if I couldn't give her that.

I take a deep breath. "I guess you know Harrison," I say.

"He's *Harrison* to you? You can't have known him for very long. And yet you're already such close friends."

He asked me to call him Harrison, probably because I'm offering such a great deal and he wants to make me feel like we're close. It's not a tactic I'm falling for, but I was happy to play into it at the time because I also want him to feel like we're buddies to make him feel at ease throughout all of this. Now, it's coming back to bite me. This makes the whole thing look worse to Pam. It looks like Harrison and I are friends who've been conspiring against her family all along. It looks like she never had a chance here.

She probably didn't. I know Matt can't compete with me financially. But there's no reason for me to rub that in.

"We're not friends," I say. "I was only trying to keep it friendly."

"*You're* the other buyer," she says. "The one he's selling to instead of Dad."

I nod. "I am." There is no point in being coy about it now.

"You don't sound surprised," she says. "I'm not telling you anything you didn't know, am I? You knew Dad was trying to buy the same parcel of land you're buying, and you didn't care. You did it anyway."

"Pam, come on," I say. "This is an opportunity for me. Did you think I moved to this part of the country because I wanted to volunteer in someone else's vineyard for the rest of my life? I want to open my own. I don't think I should have to feel ashamed of that."

"So you've been volunteering for Dad because you want to get experience and learn his techniques to apply to *your* vineyard when you open it? You've been using my father for a free education, is that it? And then you want to buy the piece of land you know for a fact he's trying to purchase, right out from under him. I can't believe you'd take advantage of my family like that!"

"It's not like I want that land *because* your father wanted it," I point out, hoping to reason with her. "I didn't even know he was the other buyer when I placed my offer. Harrison only told me because I pressed him several times."

"Of course he did. He wouldn't tell *us* who the competition was, but he told *you*. I'm sure he would tell you anything you asked him, right? Because you're such good friends. Or maybe it's your money he's in love with. Is that it?"

"No, that's not it," I snap. "You don't need to be like this. It's perfectly fair for me to buy a piece of land and open a vineyard. I'm sorry your father wanted the same piece of property. I truly am, but the fact that he wanted it doesn't make it automatically his. Besides, I thought you might be happy for me here. Your father already has a huge vineyard. Wouldn't you like me to have one too?"

"You have no idea what you're talking about," she says. She's raging, I can tell. Her voice is quiet, but her fists are clenched on the table and her jaw is tight. "What do you think is happening here? Do you think my father is buying up land because he wants to own everything? Oh no wait—I forgot. That's what *you* do, so you would think other people are doing that."

"What do you mean, that's what I do?"

"Trying to buy my cottage from under me," she says. "Trying to buy up all the property along Good Harbor Bay coastline. Hey Christos, let me ask you something. How can you say my father already has a vineyard and so he doesn't need any more land, and meanwhile you already have that big ass house and yet you're trying to buy mine? Do you hear how hypocritical you sound?"

"That's different," I say.

She snorts. "It's *not* different. It's exactly the same. You think you should get whatever you want, no matter who you stomp on to get it. You want a vineyard, so it doesn't matter that you're buying land my family has had our eye on for years. It doesn't matter that we have plans for that space that we won't make happen now because you had to have it and you know we can't compete with you."

"And why can't you do these plans of yours on the land you already have?" I ask her, raising an eyebrow. "What you have isn't good enough?"

"Oh, for God's sake. You're only proving to me that you don't have what it takes to own and operate a vineyard if you can't even understand the need for expansion."

That pisses me off. "I know you've been off at school learning how to tell one wine from another, and to pair wines with food," I tell her. "But that doesn't mean that you know more than I do about how to run a business."

"Oh fuck! It means I know more than you do about how to run *this* business. I've been involved in this business since I was a little kid. I grew up around it. Don't pretend to think that I don't know what I'm talking about. And you're nothing but a tourist who decided to hang around and, what, grow grapes on a whim? Give me a break, Christos. You're not cut out for this."

I get up from the table. "I knew this was going to be a problem," I say. "That's why I didn't tell you when I found out your father was trying to buy that land. I knew we'd have a conflict about it. I was ready to walk away if Harrison sold to your family. But I had no idea you were going to be like *this*."

"Like what?" She stands up too. "Like someone who doesn't knuckle under and tell you that you should have whatever you want, no matter what the cost to anybody else might be? You didn't think I'd stand up for myself and my family? You thought I would laugh it off, that I'd say, *oh, well, never mind my dreams, never mind everything I worked my entire life for and went to school to try to accomplish—what matters most is that my boyfriend gets his way.*"

She's never used the word *boyfriend* before, and I hate that it's happening in the middle of a fight. It also occurs to me that I don't know if that's what we are, and I don't know if that's what I want to be—not if she's going to be like this. "You yell at me for taking things I want, but aren't you the same?" I ask her. "Aren't you upset because *you* aren't getting what you want? Should I be the one to knuckle under? Roll over and say that it doesn't matter how much I might want to settle down here, open a vineyard of my own because what you want is more important?"

I've got a point, and I know I do. I'm sure she knows it too. If wanting to buy her house is the same thing as her father wanting to expand his vineyard, it stands to reason that putting my wishes ahead of hers is the same as Pam putting hers ahead of mine.

She knows it. But there's nothing she can say about it. So instead, she points to the door. "Get out," she says.

"Pam, come on. You're making this into a bigger deal than it has to be."

"You're not going to stand there and tell me I'm overreacting," she says. "Get the fuck out of my house, Christos. I'm finished with this. If you have this little regard for me, we're done. And don't bother coming back to the vineyard anymore either. Dad doesn't need you learning the ins and outs of his business while you plot to cut his legs out from under him."

She's going to tell Matt, then. And that's the end of it.

At least I can buy that land now without feeling guilty—there isn't anyone left to betray.

But as I turn and walk out of the house, that thought doesn't bring me nearly as much comfort as I'd thought it would.

Chapter 18
Pamela

The next two weeks seem to pass by in a blur.

I spend my mornings at the vineyard picking grapes and helping my father. Afternoons are spent in the tasting room, pouring and teaching the guests about our varietals, occasionally selling cases of each at a time, and helping with selections for parties, weddings, restaurants, and private wine cellars. Every minute is rife with the awareness that this is not what I'm supposed to be doing.

Part of that is that I know I was meant for bigger and better things in terms of my career. I should be pairing wines with five-star meals. I should be experimenting with new varietals, creating the new pink Riesling I've fantasized about all this time. None of that is possible, and it's all Christos' fault.

But part of my distress comes from the fact that I feel like I should be *with him*. I shouldn't be spending day after day picking grapes by myself, clearing up the tasting room at night with no one here with me. I shouldn't be falling asleep all alone in my too-big bed. My body misses him as much as anything else. It's painful, knowing that I had something so good and then lost it.

It's Sunday again. I have time to myself, and I don't want to spend it moping around the house the way I did last weekend. More than that, I don't want to walk to the beach and see Christos' big house looming over me like a shadow. I wish I could stop thinking about him. I wish

I wasn't angry at him because my anger calls him to mind so potently. I can't bring myself to think about anything else.

I keep my eyes firmly on the ground as I walk out my front door and toward town. If he's outside, I don't want to see him, and either way, I have no intention of looking over at his house. That house he already owns, so why should he need mine?

Comparing buying up residential property to buying acres of growing land was the stupidest thing he could have said. It's a thought I've had many times, but it comes back to me again as I walk up the road. Dad wants to expand the vineyard. It's a business. Does he think businesses never expand? He can't possibly be that naïve. And anyway, that's not the same thing as trying to buy a house when you already have one so that you can own all the beachfront property. He's being greedy. He can't live in two homes at the same time. All he'd be doing would be taking it away from me!

These days, I'm incredibly grateful Rose is so stubborn about selling the place. But who knows, clearly Christos had enough money to make Harrison Cooper an offer he couldn't refuse. Maybe he'll do the same to Rose. Everyone has a price. He'll find hers—and then the whole thing will be over.

I won't leave Dad. I won't leave the vineyard.

I won't—but how am I going to stay? If I'm evicted from my house, it'll mean moving back in with my father—moving in with him and working on his land for the rest of my life even though that'll never provide me the advantages and opportunities I'm looking for. Even though my life isn't going to be anything like what I hoped it would be. Even so, I'm loyal to MacLaine Winery, no matter what happens. Even if I have to move back into my childhood bedroom and spend my nights pouring the same set of wines I've got nothing new to say about.

I'm so deep in my thoughts that I hardly notice when I reach Fishtown. But suddenly I'm standing beside the harbor, looking out at the boats and recalling the last time I was here with Christos.

He's even ruined this for me. I can't stand and look at this amazing view anymore because it makes me think of him. How nice it was to do this when he was next to me. How much more beautiful it all seemed when we were together.

I was right to end things. I know that. I can't be with someone who would betray my family. But even so, I can't help missing him. I've never felt the way I did when he looked at me. I've never had such great sex in my life. No one has ever made me laugh the way he could. I think I might even have been starting to—

No. No, I won't say it. I wasn't falling in love with Christos. I won't even allow myself to think about it.

And then I turn around and get smacked in the face with the very thing I least wanted to see—or, perhaps, the thing I *most* wanted to see.

He's there.

He's right across the street from me, and there's no point in pretending we didn't see each other. He's already walking toward me. I steel myself and wait for him to draw close.

"Hey," he says.

"Hey?" A casual Hey, as if nothing happened at all? That's what I'm getting?

He sighs. "This is still happening, huh?"

"Did you think I was going to sleep on it and decide I was fine with you buying land from under my father?"

"Damn it, Pam—you act like your father already owns that land!"

"I'm not talking about this with you here. All I need is Dad to come up and see us arguing."

"Fine, then." He turns and stalks off. I watch him disappear down Lake Street towards the park. After a minute, I turn and chase after him. It's unclear if he meant me to follow, but I can't help myself—I'm not finished with this conversation.

And I guess he did want me to follow him because just as he turns onto the path towards the town beach, he wheels about to face me and seems utterly unsurprised to find me there. He opens his mouth, and I think he's about to say something. I'm already readying my retort, sure this is going to be an intense argument—

And then he grabs me and kisses me.

My mind is shocked. My heart is shocked. But my body responds thoughtlessly, and I'm kissing him back before I know what the hell I'm doing. It's the most passionate, powerful kiss the two of us have ever shared, which is saying something—it feels like whatever this is could end at any moment, and I need to grab every ounce of it while I can it's still an offer.

I wrap my arms around his neck and pull him close. My leg winds around his hip, and then his hands are under my thighs, lifting me, and I swear it's not until he's holding me in his arms with my legs firmly wrapped around his waist—it's not until I can feel the hard length of him pressed right against me that I remember I wore a skirt today.

It's almost like I knew this was going to happen.

He holds me tightly against him as we devour each other, and all I can think about is how hard he's getting. I should probably walk away from this, but I've spent the last several days worked up about the fact that leaving him meant leaving behind the best sex I've ever had. I'll be damned if I'm not going to take advantage of this opportunity now that it's presented itself—now that I can have him one more time. Maybe it isn't a good idea. No, it certainly isn't a good idea. And I don't care.

So when he sets me back on the ground, turns me to face the opposite way, and flips my skirt up to expose my ass, I don't object. I don't think about the fact that we're just a block off the middle of a tiny town, hidden only by the fact that we're down a completely public, but little-known and heavily treed pathway to the public beach. We won't be seen from the main thoroughfare, but if anyone turned down this path, they'd see everything. I don't care about that. I want that cock inside me right now.

I bend over farther, pushing my hips back toward him. He groans deep and low in his throat, and I can tell he likes what he sees.

A moment later, I feel the cool air on my skin as my panties fall to the ground around my ankles. *Fuck*.

His hand meets my ass in a gentle slap that sends a surge of arousal coursing through me. I want him so badly I could cry. The sound of his zipper has my knees shaking, and my hips buck involuntarily as if grinding against thin air is going to do anything for me.

His hand stays steady as I move against it, his fingers expertly tracing the contours of my need. He finds my clit and knows exactly where to press, and exactly how to stroke, and my whole body responds with a surge of anticipation. His touch is firm yet gentle, teasing me with just enough pressure to make me ache for more. He leans in, his breath hot against my ear, and whispers my name, sending a shiver down my spine.

His hand cups my breasts, while I rock against his palm, bending my knees to bring myself harder against him. *Oh*, it's good. I'm going to come, I—

He takes his hand away. I can't restrain my cry of dismay.

But then he's back, his hips *finally* flush against mine, pushing into me. His hands grip the tops of my thighs and he fucks me hard, punishingly harder, and now I know I am going to come, there's no fucking stopping it. His hand claps over my mouth barely in time to catch my cries of ecstasy as I lose myself in pleasure.

I go limp as my orgasm subsides. He cradles me in his arms like a rag doll against his body, still fucking me hard. The moment before he comes, I feel his thighs tremble, and I wish I was facing him so that I could kiss him, but I know I shouldn't want that. Common sense is rushing back and it's coming far too fast.

He slams into me hard when he comes. I know the moment he pulls away we will go back to not speaking to each other, and maybe he knows it too, because he lingers inside me for a moment, obviously reluctant for this moment to end.

It has to.

He withdraws from me, and I feel so fucking empty.

"I should go," he says softly, letting his hand rest on my shoulder for a long moment. It's enough to make me feel things could still be okay between us, even though I know it's only an illusion. But he can't disguise the fact that he cares about me.

I can't pretend I don't care about him.

He should go. And so should I.

The silence hangs heavy between us, each clinging to the lingering touch as if it could somehow bridge the gap that is now a reality. His eyes search mine, and for a fleeting moment, it feels like we could find our way back to each other, but reality presses down. I want to stay, the ache of what could be makes it all the harder to let go.

I can't stand that it has to be like this.

Chapter 19
Pamela

"Brian!"

I can't believe my brother is finally here. I sprint across the living room of Dad's house and fling my arms around him. He catches me in the embrace with a laugh. "Jeez, Pam. You'd think we hadn't seen each other in two years."

I slug his arm with a laugh because we *haven't* seen each other in two years. "It's been too damn long," I tell him. "I was so annoyed when I realized you would be out of town when I got back!"

"Yeah, I didn't like it either," he says. "But it had to be done. Business is business."

"And speaking of business," Dad says, entering the room. "Now that you're both here, we need a family meeting."

"Dad, come on," Brian says with a laugh. "I've been back in town for what, half an hour? Do you want to get down to business? Can't we take tonight to be a family?"

"No, Dad's right," I tell Brian. "We've got a serious problem on our hands." A serious problem who just had his dick inside me an hour ago, but that particular aspect of the problem isn't for my family to know to help me with. "Did Dad already tell you?"

"He told me we aren't going to be able to make the land purchase we wanted."

"Right," Dad says. "Because of *someone's boyfriend*."

"Dad, stop," I say. "You know I ended it when I found out."

"Hang on." Brian holds up both hands. "Someone needs to catch me up on something here."

"She was dating Chris, or *Christos* to her," Dad says. "Not that I would have put it in those terms. I'd say he was using her to get close to the family."

"And I've asked you not to talk about it like that," I say firmly. I don't think Dad is *entirely* wrong—Christos was trying to get in with our family, to find out how to run a winery. That much is obvious. But I don't think that's the only reason we were together. Dad would like it to be that way, and there's a part of me that would like that too, because it would be easier to write Christos off if I could think of him as a manipulative, terrible person who never cared about me. But I don't believe that's the truth. He did care.

He cared about other things more, though. He never cared about me as much as I thought he should have. If he *had* cared enough, he and I would still be together. We would have worked out a solution to the land problem that had a chance at making everybody happy.

That's probably a pipe dream. It probably never could have been done.

"Back up," Brian says. "You were dating my friend, Dad's friend, Chris– I mean *Christos*?"

"It's not like how Dad is making it sound. We were just getting to know each other," I say. "Then I found out he was trying to buy the land we need, and when I called him out on it, he refused to back off, so I ended things with him. It's that simple."

"You shouldn't have had anything to do with him in the first place," Dad says. "I did warn you."

"Can you not, with the *I told you so*?"

"I did tell you so."

"Dad, hold on," Brian says. "This is the same Chris we're talking about. We like him."

"We don't like him *now*," I say.

"We're, what, cutting him off completely because we found out he was trying to buy the same property we are? Aren't *we* also trying to buy the same property *he* is?"

"Now you sound like him," I say.

"I could do worse. Chris – I mean Christos - is a decent guy."

"He's a con man," Dad says bluntly. "I should never have let him volunteer on the vineyard. I should have known when he offered to work for free that something was up."

"You're not letting him volunteer anymore?" Brian asks. "He's been such a tremendous help to us, Dad, come on. Don't you think you're overreacting a bit here? Did Harrison actually sell him the property?"

"Not yet. And I'm not overreacting at all," Dad snaps. "I'm doing what has to be done to protect our family and our business."

Brian makes eye contact with me and cocks his head sideways. I know what he's doing. Our unspoken sibling communication has always been great, and I know he's trying to send a message *"Isn't Dad being unreasonable?"*

But I don't return his look, because I don't agree. Dad's not being unreasonable. My feelings about Christos are complicated as hell, but when it comes to how he's interacted with us on a business level it's simple. He's been awful, he's taken advantage of us, and I won't forgive that any time soon.

I turn away from Brian. He huffs out a frustrated sigh and I can tell he thinks we're being silly, but I don't care. He wasn't here when this happened. He doesn't know how it felt to have to look in the eyes of someone I was insanely close to, and then to realize that he'd never cared for me the way I did for him, that what he cared about most was getting his hands on that land—and he didn't mind that he had to kill my dreams to do it.

Fucking him down the boardwalk is one thing, but Dad's right. We can't ever let him back into the business. Trusting him is the biggest mistake we could have made, and I consider us lucky that the outcome wasn't any worse. At least all we're losing is the potential future of our business. Now that I've seen Christos' true colors, I wouldn't have any trouble believing he'd put us out of business entirely if he thought it would serve his end.

Fuck, it kills me that I have such strong feelings for him and yet at the same time I can't stand him. I don't know how to manage the tension between those two things.

Brian seems to believe it should be easier than it is. I usually trust my brother's judgment, but he's got it wrong. Dad's the one who has it right, who understands the depths of Christos' betrayal of us all. Maybe Brian will get it once he's been home a bit longer. He needs to see Christos to understand the extent of it. A conversation between the two of them will make things clear to Brian.

All I know is that I don't want Christos anywhere near my family's business. He's done enough.

Chapter 20
Christos

I know what the ringing phone is about before I answer it - the line to my home office is a number few people have. This is no call from Harrison Cooper. I've been brooding about Pamela and what's going on between us, but the moment that phone rings, it drives all those thoughts out of my mind. This is far more important.

I grab it, reaching for a notepad, because I know I'll have to write things down. "Christos Tzavaras speaking."

The voice on the other end is all business. There are no pleasantries, just a quick walk-through of details. I scratch them all down on my notepad—the location of the job, the details of what's going on. It will be a tough one, I can tell that already, but I'm up for it. I always am.

When I've gotten all the information, I thank my contact and hang up the phone. I've been doing this for years, back to my active SEAL days, but it still surprises me how easy it is to keep a cool, clear head at times like this. I'm not anxious about the job at all. I'm not worried about what could happen, even though I know this is dangerous. I'm thinking only about what has to be done and my next steps to accomplish it.

I don't know what country we're going to—that's a part of this, every time. I can't know. It's part of what makes it okay for the military to fly in our little private team to deal with situations like this—they keep some things confidential. They'll give us the information, and the pilot will know where we're going, but he won't be a government pilot, and we won't be on a US military plane. We won't find out where we are until we land, maybe not even then.

But there's one thing I do know—one thing that's consistently true every time something like this happens. We'll be landing in enemy territory. The reason we have to do this, the reason the army can't, is that for the US military to get involved would be an act of aggression and could provoke a serious international incident. It's not exactly risk-free on that score for a private group to go in, but it's a lot less risky. If something goes wrong, the government has plausible deniability. But that's why they pay us so fucking much. I call it stupid money. But every mission is worth it. My specialized tactical equipment can never be tracked back to the government. They can condemn our actions as a rogue and prevent conflict from breaking out.

That's one of the many things I could never have said to Pamela, even if we stayed together. Hearing that the government is going to deny responsibility for you if you get caught...that's something that's bound to scare civilians. It doesn't scare me—not anymore. I take it as a matter of course now. But I know it would have freaked her out, and it probably should.

I pick the phone up and press one of the programmed speed dial buttons. A moment later, my buddy Craig connects. "What's up?" he asks.

"Mission," I say.

"What do we know?"

"Same as usual, not much. Sounds like it's a hostage situation, but that's all I've got. Wheels up in two hours. Can you be at the airstrip?"

"Do you need me to contact the others?"

"Yes," I say. "Run the call chain." He'll call Brad, and Brad will call his contact, and on and on down the chain until everyone knows. "Be quick about it. And don't tell anyone else."

"How can I? I don't even know where we're going." Of course, Craig knows not to tell. This isn't his first rodeo. But we always remind each other anyway, because it helps to have little familiar touchstones at a time like this. Routines make the whole thing seem more digestible and less alarming. It helps to break the day down into one task at a time. My first task was to call Craig. Now I've got to grab my go bag and get down to the airstrip. My major equipment is already there in a secure underground locker.

It's about an hour's journey to get to the place where the plane will take off. As soon as I'm in my car, I feel locked in mentally. I run through the items I know are in my go bag, reminding myself that I've got enough packed to see me through whatever lies ahead. I concentrate on what I need to do to complete this mission.

The risk to my life is secondary here. We're looking at a hostage situation, and right now, my team and I are the only ones who can intercede.

I pull onto the airstrip. It's one we've used before—there are several we have access to—and I'm familiar with it. I know where to leave my car. I park and lock it. I drop my keys in a safe deposit box all the guys will use. It doesn't make sense to carry them with us. I never feel like a mission is properly over until I've taken my keys back out of the box at the end of it. That's when I let myself believe I'll be going home.

Craig's already at the airstrip when I get out of my car, which is no surprise since he lives closer than I do. I jog over to meet him. "Anybody else here yet?"

"Not yet," he says. "I got the phone chain working, so I imagine everyone will show their faces soon. Do you know what we're walking into?"

"I know we're dealing with a hostage situation," I say. "A group of very rich, and very connected teenage tourists. That's all I know."

"Someone's got to teach tourists how to handle themselves abroad," Craig says, shaking his head. "This happens too often."

"It would probably help if we had any freedom to talk about it when it did happen," I say. "No one ever hears these stories. We have to keep them so under wraps, that people keep making the same mistakes."

Craig nods. I know he finds that as frustrating as I do, but we can't do anything about it. Confidential is confidential.

I'm aware, in the back of my mind, that what's happening now has released me from the near-constant stress of thinking about Pamela, worrying that she'll never forgive me, feeling angry that I even want her forgiveness when nothing I did was serious enough to warrant the reaction she gave me. I'm tired of thinking about those things, and thanks to the current situation, I can't think about them. I can only afford to keep my mind in the present moment, on the job I have to do. Dwelling on problems with your girlfriend—or whatever Pamela is to me—is a good way to get yourself killed in the field.

The pilot comes trotting out to the small plane we take on operations like this one. He nods to me and Craig, saying nothing, and climbs into the plane to do his pre-flight check. This is standard. We don't talk about missions to anyone on the outside, not even the pilot who flies us in. He isn't going to tell us where we're going, and we aren't going to tell him what we're doing there. Secrecy has become so routine that it doesn't even register in our thoughts.

We grab our technical gear from the bunker and load it onto the plane. I jog back and forth on the tarmac while I wait. After a while, Craig begins to do the same. It's the best way to release nervous energy that I know of, and by the time the rest of the team arrives, I'm in a calm and ready state. We board the plane and take our seats, and I immediately lean back and close my eyes, focusing on relaxing my body. The exercise truly helps—I bring my heart rate down slowly, gradually, and consistently until I know I'll be able to drop off to sleep at any moment.

Before I do, I let myself listen in on the conversation going on around me. The other guys are calm too. They've all got their pre-mission rituals, ways of getting in the zone. Some of them are leaving behind wives and children. I've never understood how they were able to do that. I've never thought I'd leave behind someone who meant that much to me. Maybe that's why I've never let anyone get that close—it would force me to make a choice.

Now, sitting on this plane, I see how easy it is. Even if Pamela and I hadn't split up I would do this. Even if I knew she was waiting anxiously for me at home, I could handle it.

For a nanosecond, I thought, maybe I couldn't.

Maybe it's for the best that I don't have to find out. I should thank her for ending things when she did. It's probably made my life easier.

Then again, when did I become someone who wanted an easy life? That's never been who I am.

I don't know what to think, so I let myself relax into sleep. When I wake up, we'll be there, and I'll have my thoughts centered entirely on the mission. Right now, it seems like the perfect distraction.

Chapter 21
Pamela

It's been a month since Brian returned to town, and still, no one has seen or heard from Christos.

I know what this means, of course.

At first, I thought maybe he was avoiding me. At first, I was even glad of it, because after what happened the last time we saw each other, I'm not sure I could count on myself to keep my distance from him. I don't think I can trust myself around him—the next time I see him, I'll probably jump all over him again. And as much fun as that was, it isn't a good idea.

Still, I think the anxiety of knowing that he's almost surely off on some military mission is starting to get to me, because my breasts miss him, and I've been feeling nauseous for days. I wish I could relax, but I can't do it.

I'm pouring myself a glass of Merlot, hoping it'll take the edge off when the obvious thought finally occurs to me.

My nausea doesn't have anything to do with Christos. My breasts are *tender*, fuck- they don't *miss* him.

My nausea doesn't have anything to do with his absence.

I know I shouldn't jump to conclusions here. But as soon as the thought occurs to me, I *know* I'm right. Taking the test will be a formality. I know instinctively, biologically, as surely as I know that blood is flowing through my veins without needing science to check my body and prove it so.

I'm pregnant.

The math checks out. I haven't had a period since I came back to the US. I can't believe I didn't notice that until now—but, it's not so surprising, given everything else that's happened. It was the furthest thing from my mind, but it isn't now.

I'm glad the local drugstore delivers. I place an order with other things and sit down to wait. The twenty minutes it takes for the pregnancy test to reach me feels more like an hour, and I wish to God that I could drink that Merlot, but I know I shouldn't. Not while there's this possibility. I pour it out into the sink instead, with a pang of regret—that was an exceptional bottle, and now the whole thing is going to waste.

There's a knock on the door. *Thank God.* I run to open it.

But the person on the other side isn't my delivery driver. It's my brother Brian. Of course - it's a small town. He's holding the bag from the drugstore, and the expression on his face tells me beyond doubt that he's looked inside.

Shit.

"Well, you might as well come in," I say, feeling hopeless. I reach out for the bag and he hands it to me wordlessly. I close the door behind him. "What are you doing here?" I ask.

"I came to see you," Brian says. "I wanted to talk to you—about this business with Dad and Chris*tos*." He says the end of Christos' name with an air of annoyance. "I thought we could get on the same side about it while Christos is out of town—"

He's still staring at the bag in my hand. We won't make progress on this conversation until we address the elephant in the room.

"I don't know yet," I say, in response to his unspoken question. "I still have to take the test."

"But—Christos would be the father?"

"Of course, Brian, who else?"

"I had to ask," he says defensively. "Does he know?"

"How could he know? None of us have seen or heard from him in weeks."

"I don't know. You're the one who was dating him. Maybe you have some way of contacting him that Dad and I don't know about. Maybe you two have been talking all this time."

"Well, let me get my Bat-phone out—hell no we haven't," I say with sarcasm and a sigh. "And even if we had, I haven't said anything to him. I don't even know whether or not there's anything to tell yet."

"But you think there is."

"I have to take the test," I repeat.

"Don't let me stop you."

"You want me to do it now, with you here?"

"Do you want me to leave?" he counters.

And his point is taken, because I don't want that. I'm already feeling freaked out and alone. Having my brother here will make me feel better, and will make this easier to handle, even if it does feel weird to take a pregnancy test with him in the next room.

"Wait here," I say. I glance at the kitchen. "There's an open bottle of Merlot, I don't think I'm going to drink it now. You're welcome to it if you want it. It will probably go to waste otherwise."

Brian nods and I head into the bathroom.

Three minutes later, I'm staring at the plus sign on the test stick and wondering how I got into this mess. This is the result I expected, but, now that I'm looking at it, it feels like the least likely thing in the world.

I put the test down on the edge of the sink, feeling like it might break, and walk out into the living room.

Brian knows right away. He must be reading it on my face or something, but I can tell he knows. "Shit."

I take a deep breath and sit in the chair opposite him, wondering what the hell I'm going to do now. How can I be having a baby with a man I'm barely speaking to? But on the other hand—how can I have a baby at all? Of all the things I thought my life would bring me when I came back home from France, this wasn't even on my radar. I can't believe it's happening.

"Hey," Brian says soothingly.

I look up. While I was lost in thought, I guess he went to the kitchen and got a glass of water for me. I take it from him gratefully and take a long swallow. I'm still in shock about this.

"What are you going to do?" Brian asks gently.

"I haven't even thought about that."

"I'll support you, you know. No matter what."

I'm wildly grateful he's here. "I guess I'm going to have a baby," I say because even though I haven't spent time thinking about it, anything else seems incomprehensible. Motherhood was always part of the long-term plan. I never imagined it would look anything like *this*, and about ten other things were supposed to happen first—but I guess life never happens according to plan. This is what the universe is serving me today, so I'll take it.

I'm expecting Brian to give me some big, elaborate argument, to tell me that I haven't thought this through and I'm making an emotional decision. Maybe I am doing that. But if I am, my brother doesn't call me out. He nods. "Okay."

"That's it? *Okay?*"

"I mean, Dad's probably going to flip out. But if this is what you want, I'm here for you." Then he adds with a hint of a smile, "I'm gonna be an uncle."

I feel my eyes welling up with tears. This could have been so much worse. As hard as it is to face, I could have been stuck trying to go through it all by myself, with no one at all for support. I'm so thankful for my brother right now.

"Do you want me to come with you when you tell Christos?" Brian asks.

I blink. "Christos isn't even here."

"But he'll be back. He always comes back." Brian pauses. "You are planning on telling him, aren't you?"

"I don't know if I can."

"You can. Pamela, you have to," Brian says. "He's going to find out, you know. He's your neighbor. Even if you don't tell him anything, he'll see you. He'll figure it out eventually. Wouldn't you rather he heard it from you than to find out like that—or for some neighborhood gossip to fill him in once *they* find out? You know how small Fishtown is, everybody knows you and Christos have been dating. I know it will be awkward as hell, but you've got to be the one to tell him. There's no good outcome if you keep it to yourself."

I suppose he's right. "It's only the idea of a conversation with Christos right now—I can't think of anything I want to do less than that."

And again, I'm flashing back to the last time he and I spoke to one another. It won't be like that this time. The idea would be laughable if I were in the mood for laughing. As it is, it pushes me closer than ever to crying.

Brian pulls me out of my chair and wraps his arms around me. It feels so good to let my brother hug me for a moment. There's such security and familiarity in it and for the moment things don't seem so bad. I have my family, and I know they'll be on my side no matter what. It doesn't matter what Christos has to say about any of this. It doesn't matter if he does or doesn't find out, or how he feels about it when that happens.

But of course, that's not true. I do care what Christos thinks. I've never stopped caring about him. He's gone now, and I know where he is—off on one of those dangerous missions he told me about, those missions that he can't tell me or anyone else where he's going or what he's doing or when to expect him back—anything. I don't know if I'll ever see him again. Maybe he'll be in his house tomorrow, and it will be as if he was never gone. Or maybe he'll never come home again and I'll always have to wonder what happened to him.

How could I have ever thought I could date a man who lived like that? No matter how much I cared about him—and I did care about him, I won't deny that—how could I go through times like this one, wondering if he was coming home? How much worse would this be if we were in a relationship? If the *three* of us were a family?

No, it's good we separated. It's good our lives got in the way of us being together.

Brian is right. If he comes home, I'll tell him something. I'll figure that out when the time comes, though.

If it ever does.

Chapter 22
Christos

"Take this *slowly*," I breathe to Craig through our comms, barely above a whisper.

Craig nods, lifts himself up on his toes, and peers in the window right above us. Then he drops back down and gives me a nod.

They're here, all right.

I signal the rest of the team, who are waiting at the end of the alley, and they jog around to take their positions around the perimeter of the building. They'll be guarding the exits—all the doors and windows—so that no one can run out and escape from us. Now that we've found these guys, we don't want them to get away.

"How many?" I ask him quietly.

He's looking at the readout from our surveillance equipment on the device in his hand. "Heat signatures say four. Two of those will be the hostages."

Okay. That's good. That means it will be fine for the two of us to go in on our own, without calling for anybody else. I'd prefer to leave the rest of the team outside. It's a big building, and I don't want to take the chance of leaving any part of it unguarded while we do this.

I point to the door.

Craig nods.

I point to myself, then to him, to indicate the order we should go inside.

Craig frowns. I know what he's thinking—he doesn't want to send me in first. He'd rather do that part. I understand that because I'm the same way. If someone's going to run into danger, I don't want it to be a member of my team. I want it to be me.

Unfortunately for Craig, I outrank him, so this isn't his call. Besides, this was all discussed on the plane on the way over, and if there's one thing we don't do, it's change the plan in the field when we don't need to. Craig's far too skilled and professional to do that, even if he does want to go in first.

I place my magnetic bolt laser on the door where I estimate the deadbolt will be. The laser lights up red for a second, then green, letting me know it has run through the bolt and severed it. The door will now be unlocked.

"Go time," I murmur into my comm, and Craig and I move toward the door. I push it open and lead the way inside, weapon up.

The hostages—two young women in their early twenties—are sitting on the floor. Their hands are zip-tied and they look haggard and terrified. I wish I could go right to them, grab them, and get them out of here, but I've got my focus on their captors. The two men in the room have been drinking, so they aren't ready for this at all, and that's perfect. One of them immediately starts shouting at me in Russian, and that's ideal because the whole team knows Russian—it's one of the languages we've learned as part of our training. I've got my gun on them in no time. Craig is at my back, and I'm confident this mission will be quick. Everything's going perfectly.

"Put your hands up," I order the men, also in Russian.

They look at each other, then look back at me.

"I know you can understand me," I tell the men. "Put your fucking hands up."

They lift their hands slowly into the air. Craig goes over to them and pats them down quickly. "They're clean," he informs me.

"Untie the girls," I tell him. "And secure those two."

I wish we had jurisdiction to arrest them, to bring charges against them, but this isn't our country and we aren't even supposed to be here, officially. There's nothing we can do to them. The key is to grab the girls and get out of here before they figure out we have no middle ground between threats and shooting. There's nothing to do to escalate this, apart from the most extreme option. And I would prefer to get out of here without killing anyone if I can.

Craig lowers his gun slowly, his eyes on the men as he moves toward them to secure them, making sure they aren't going to try anything. I'm pretty confident that they won't. They seem completely blown away by our presence, which makes sense given that they have no context to explain who we are, how we found them, or by what authority we've come bursting into their little safe-house. Nothing about us identifies us as US Military, by design, we could be anybody. I know that has the potential to make us seem a lot scarier. There are limits to what the military will do. There are lines they won't cross. I won't cross those lines either—I'm not about to commit any war crimes here—but these guys don't know me and don't know how far I'd be willing to go.

The men are now secured. Craig kneels beside the girls, cuts their zip ties, and helps them to their feet. The fact that they're able to stand is promising. In a situation like this, there's always a concern victims need to be carried out, and that would be a problem because it would require both of us to secure our weapons.

"Head out," I tell Craig, still communicating in Russian.

"What about you?"

"I'm right behind you," I assure him. Everything has gone smoothly today, and we're almost out of here. I won't hang around and push my luck, even though part of me would love to rough these guys up before I go. We've been lucky here. I can't take a chance on things going south.

I'm backing up toward the door we came in through. Craig and the girls are behind me, and I'm covering our retreat with my weapon, making sure the two men in front of me don't make a move.

My eyes are so glued to their faces that I don't even notice when one of the men makes a move with his foot.

Craig lets out a yell. I'm trained to respond to distress in my partner's voice, and my reaction is instant and almost involuntary. "Get them out!" I call, just as I was turning toward the door, knowing that despite all our efforts, something went wrong.

I see the tripwire on the floor that the man is moving toward a moment before he reaches it. I see the venom in his eyes. And then I feel an explosion of pain in my gut as I returned fire.

Spring-gun. A shotgun blast rang out.

My rational mind is processing all this even as the pain begins to mount in intensity. It was something I could never have planned for—a shot from that angle, under my bulletproof vest.

It's so intense that I don't even have any extra space in my mind to worry about the mission or to remember, more than fleetingly, that a stomach wound is one of the worst you can take from a bullet. I'm not even thinking about the fact that this might kill me. All I can think about is the pain.

Craig will get the girls out. I know he will. That's what's most important. Even if one of our people takes a hit, the priority is always to save the hostages. He knows that. He won't forget it now.

For a fraction of a second, I feel a spike of fear, jabbing through the pain, because what if I can't make it back to the plane? The guys would never leave me behind, but what happens if they don't get me out in time? I'm going to die on foreign soil with no one who knows where I am. No one will know what happened to me. No—Craig will know, the team will know—but will they tell Pamela?

Pamela.

Fuck, I shouldn't have left things the way I did with her. I should have let her know what she meant to me. Hell, maybe I should have let her family have that land. Now I'll never see her again, and she'll never know how much I cared about her...

"Stay with me, Chris."

I recognize the voice. It's Craig. I knew he'd be back. I open my mouth, trying to tell him he shouldn't be here, he needs to get the hostages out, but all that comes out is a groan.

"It's okay," Craig says. "Everything's under control. We're about to move you out, but we have a long flight ahead of us, so hang tight."

The world is spinning around me, which I'm grateful for because the pain is less intense. I feel like passing out. Craig said to stay with him, but it's too much. My eyes are heavy and start to close, the darkness sweeps in from the edges and starts to overcome me. Fuck, I can't be dying.

Before I give in to it, my last thought is of Pamela. I wonder where she is right now. I wonder if she's all right. And when she hears what happened to me, how will she react?

I don't want her to be sad.

But I hope she'll miss me.

Chapter 23
Pamela

"You know you can't keep sitting around the house like this," Brian says. "Come on over to the tasting room."

"I don't want to." I know I'm being sulky and unpleasant, but I can't manage to focus on anything but how unhappy I am right now.

It's been two weeks since I discovered my pregnancy, and there's still no word from Christos. What am I supposed to do? It's hard to believe that I ever had doubts about whether I should tell him—I want to tell him. I'm dying to tell him. And I don't know if I'm going to see him again.

"You have to get out of the house," Brian insists. "I know this is about Christos."

"Of course, it's about him. He's been gone for ages."

"He does this. You knew that, Pam. He disappears. But he always comes back."

"Has he ever been gone this long?" I ask hopelessly.

I already know what the answer is going to be, and Brian doesn't say it. "He'll be back," he says.

His tone is reassuring, and I wish I could ignore the evidence of my senses and trust what my brother is saying. But it doesn't feel like Christos is going to come back. I know he's gone off to do something dangerous, and there's no one in my life I can talk to about this who can tell me where he went. And given that he's been gone as long as he has...

I mean, who would contact me if something happened to him? Who am I to him? Dad and Brian are the only people who know that Christos and I are part of each other's lives, and they can't tell me anything. His team wouldn't know to reach out to me, and if he has family, they don't know who I am. I'm literally having his baby, and no one in the world would even think to tell me what happened to him. The thought is devastating.

I can't leave the house. Not under these conditions. Who the hell could?

"Leave me alone," I tell Brian, ashamed that I'm talking to him like that when he's been so supportive. But maybe he understands that I need to be upset about this because he squeezes my shoulder and leaves without another word.

Once alone in the house, I bury my face in my hands and sit still, waiting for something to happen. Something to lift me out of my current mood—or, if not that, for enough time to pass that I don't feel so distressed anymore. Because surely, eventually, this isn't going to hurt as much as it does right now. There will be a day when I'm able to smile again. But it's hard to imagine that right now.

Even though my baby isn't a baby yet—it's the size of a pea—it feels like the two of us are all each other has in the world. I put my hands on my stomach and imagine the baby knows I'm here. It feels like I'm letting it down by not being in contact with its father, even though I know that isn't my fault. I hate that this is happening. My child is going to be fatherless. It makes everything so much more painful. So much worse.

I try to convince myself to get up, take a shower, get dressed, and go to the vineyard. Brian is right—I can't stop living my life because this is happening. Eventually, I have to figure out a way to go on. I also have to let Dad know I'm having a baby. I don't think he'll be wild about the idea once he finds out who the father is, but he'll have to know eventually, and I'd rather rip the bandage off. Brian offered to tell him for me, but I know I've got to do it myself. It's hard, but I have to be strong here. I'm going to be doing this on my own, I guess.

But I can't make myself get up. I can't bring myself to face it. One more day of lying in bed with the covers pulled over my head—I can allow myself that. I'll get up and go back to work tomorrow. I'll tell Dad what's going on then.

I'm about to get up to lie down in my room when the phone rings.

I'm sure it's going to be Brian. I'm sure he's calling to tell me that he hasn't given up on getting me out of the house, he's on his way back over to try to take me out. He'll probably offer a coffee run or something low-stress like that—something where I can stay in the car, but I'll have to be exposed to fresh air.

I'll go with him. I've already decided. I've done enough feeling sorry for myself. Whatever's happened to Christos, I'll find out eventually—hell, Rose will probably be able to tell me, if nothing else. She finds out all the gossip.

I reach for the phone and glance at the image on the screen.

I swear to God, my heart nearly stops beating.

It's not Brian. The call is coming from Christos.

I'm in shock, I let the phone ring several more times before I get my act together and answer it. "Hello?" My voice is shaking. If I'd gotten this call a week ago, I would have answered it with a demand for information or an explanation. Now I'm afraid that if I push too hard, this lifeline I'm being thrown will evaporate.

"Is this Pamela MacLaine?"

It's not Christos' voice on the other end. It belongs to a woman, and I don't recognize her. Something strange happens to my heart—it's dropping into my stomach. I'm suddenly filled with a nameless dread.

"Yes," I say, hardly able to breathe. "This is Pamela."

"Are you next of kin to Christos Tzavaras?"

"I'm a friend..." *Oh no.*

"Pamela, my name is Molly Cummings," the woman said. "I'm a nurse at Grace Memorial Hospital in Chicago."

"Chicago?" I swear, I cannot make all these pieces fit together. I have no idea what's happening.

"Mr. Tzavaras is a patient here," Molly explains. "He was transferred in today."

"Transferred—from where?" I have no idea why this is my first question. I have too many questions to count. This is the one that makes it out of my mouth.

"I'm afraid I don't have that information," Molly says. "All I know is that he was at another hospital."

"What's wrong with him?"

"He has a serious gunshot wound."

"*What?*"

"Surgery was performed and he's in stable condition, but he's been unconscious since the surgery. We're not sure what to expect right now. I've been trying to find someone to contact, and you were the most recent call on his phone."

"We—we're friends, like I said..." I'm shaking a little. "Is there something I can do?"

"You're welcome to come to the hospital and sit with him here if you'd like to," Molly says. "He's on his own, and if he wakes up—"

"*If* he wakes up?"

Her voice is very gentle. "We aren't sure what to expect right now. As I said, he is in stable condition, which is encouraging. But we would have hoped to see him awake before now. We're monitoring him closely. If you'd like, I'm happy to call you with daily updates or to let you know if anything changes. Or perhaps you can give me the contact information for someone else I should be talking to?"

"No," I say, my heart beating fast. "No, I'm coming to Chicago. I'll be on the next flight I can get." There's no question in my mind—this is what I want to do. "If he wakes up, will you tell him I'm on my way? I'll be there as soon as I can."

"I'll let him know," Molly says. "When you get here, you can come to the reception desk on the first floor. I'll make sure they know to expect you, and someone will bring you up to Mr. Tzavaras, even if it's outside visiting hours."

I'm sure it will be outside visiting hours by the time I get there. "Thank you," I tell her.

"Of course."

I hang up the phone. I'm shocked, but even so, I'm moving quickly, grabbing a few clothes and throwing them in a backpack. I won't try to look for plane tickets from home, I'll go to the airport and sort it out there.

I sling the backpack over my shoulder and grab my car keys. Even driving to the airport will be an ordeal with my mind the way it is, but I have to get there. I have to be with Christos. If he never wakes up from this, if the last conversation we had was the last one we'll ever get to have, I don't think I'll ever forgive myself.

I have to make things right between us, and I have to tell him about his baby.

I need to be by his side.

I need him to wake up.

Chapter 24
Christos

The air smells overly clean. Antiseptic. It feels off.

I hear low voices and something beeping steadily.

There's a dull throbbing in my abdomen—and that's when I remember that my last thoughts were of a much sharper pain, and my eyes fly open.

I'm in a hospital bed.

And the first thing I observe—with a rush of relief—is that this place is deeply, thoroughly American. There's a TV on in the corner of the room—it's on mute, but it's playing a baseball game. Two familiar teams, both of which make me feel right at home. There's a bottle of soda on the table in front of the TV and a fast-food bag with a label I recognize.

And there's a nurse in the room. She's facing away from me, writing something I can't make out on a whiteboard mounted to the wall—but she's humming a pop song that's been playing at my local grocery store all summer.

I'm home.

The nurse turns around. Her eyes widen. "Mr. Tzavaras! You're awake! Oh, goodness, that's a nice surprise. How do you feel? Do you remember what happened?"

"I was shot," I manage. My voice sounds as hoarse as a two-pack-a-day smoker's. "I was shot on the—" I catch myself before I say the word *mission*. I don't know what's going on and I don't know how I came to be back in the US, but I do know that I can't let this nurse know where I was or what I was doing. Confidentiality is the most important part of our job.

But my immediate thought is for Craig, for the rest of my team, and the two young women we went in to save. "Did anyone come in with me?" I ask.

"You were alone," the nurse says sympathetically. "But someone has arrived to see you since then."

"Craig?"

"It's a woman. She went to the cafeteria—she didn't want to leave your side. I had to talk her into it. She's been sitting here for the past forty-eight hours, waiting for you to wake up, saying things in your ear— you'd have to ask her. I'm not sure what she was talking about. Something to do with a piece of land."

My heart skips a beat. "Pamela?"

"Yes, I think that's her name," the nurse says. "My supervisor called her to let her know you were here. I haven't spoken to her myself—at least, not until today. She'll be disappointed she wasn't here when you woke up! But your vitals haven't changed, so I wasn't expecting anything to happen."

"Pamela is *here*?" I'm still stuck on that. I can't believe she's here. "Why is she here?"

"Like I said, my supervisor got in touch with her. She found her number in your phone." The nurse looks at me closely. "She *is* a friend of yours, isn't she?"

That's one way to put it. "She is," I agree. "I didn't expect her to be here, that's all."

"She's been very worried about you," the nurse explains. "I'm sure she'll be back soon, and the two of you will have a chance to—ah, here she is now.

Sure enough, the door opens and Pamela comes in. When she sees me, she drops the apple she's holding on the floor. "Christos! Oh my God—you're awake! Are you all right?"

"I was about to perform an exam to find out the answer to that question," the nurse says. "Would you like her to step out for the exam, Mr. Tzavaras? Or should she stay?"

"She can stay," I say. The nurse quickly takes my vitals and performs a few other tests. She declares me "doing well," then steps out of the room, promising to return in her next rounds.

I haven't taken my eyes off Pamela since she walked into the room. I can't believe she's here. "Why did you come?" I ask her.

"You have no idea how worried I was," she says. "I've been going out of my mind, Christos. Anything could have happened to you. You might have been dead."

"I thought I was," I admit.

She lets out an unhappy hiss. "I hate your job," she informs me miserably.

That reminds me of my other concern. "My teammates," I say. "Are they here? Did they make it back?"

"They aren't here," she says. "I told them to go home to their families—I would stay with you. But everyone's all right. And Craig told me to tell you that the status was blue—I don't know what that means."

I breathe a sigh of relief. "It means our mission was a success," I explain.

"And you aren't going to tell me what the mission was."

"No," I say. "Pamela—I can't. I'm so sorry. I wish I could—"

"Hey, no." she comes over and sits on the edge of my bed, taking my hand in hers. "You don't need to worry about that," she says. "I know you can't talk about it. I don't expect you to. I wish you could, but that isn't the way things are. I get it. I'm glad you're home safe. That's enough for me."

Her eyes are filled with tears. I squeeze her hand. "I *am* all right," I tell her. "The nurse checked me out and confirmed it. You were right there. Remember that?"

"Of course," she says. "Of course, I remember. But, Christos, you can't imagine what it was like for me these past few weeks. I've been a wreck. I thought you were lying dead somewhere, and that I would never find out about it. I thought we—I mean, I thought *I* was going to have to spend the rest of my life with that question in my mind. Can you imagine how haunting that was—not knowing if I'd ever talk to you again, wondering if you might be dead? I thought I was losing my mind, Christos. These have been the worst weeks of my life."

God, I want to sit up and take her in my arms! But the pain is still intense, but it's nowhere near what it was when I was first shot. I must have been given some painkillers, because if I had surgery then I ought to be suffering more than this.

I'm so glad to see Pamela. I don't think I've ever been happier to see someone's face in all my life.

"Hey, don't try to move," she says as I try to sit up a little bit. "Do you want me to call the nurse back to help you?"

"I don't need any help."

She smiles, but her smile is shaky and weak, and I can see it's costing her. "You don't have to do that," I tell her, trying to be reassuring. "You don't have to smile. It's okay."

That breaks her. Tears come pouring down her cheeks. It physically hurts that I can't hold her right now.

"I have to tell you something," she says. "I know it isn't the time. I should wait until you're recovered. But I almost lost you, and...I have to tell you now."

"Tell me what?"

She takes a deep breath. "I'm pregnant."

I feel the air rush out of my lungs as if I had been punched. "What?"

"I'm sorry," she says, wiping her tears. "I would have told you long ago, but you weren't here."

"You would have told me a long time ago? How long have you known?"

"A month."

My head spins. "You've been on your own with this all that time?"

"Not entirely," she says. "I had Brian. He knows. He's been so supportive, and he's been telling me all along that I needed to tell you. I know I needed to, but it was hard to feel like that when I found out. You and I had been arguing, and it felt like things were not right between us. I should have had more faith in you—well, I should have known that no matter what your reaction was, you had a right to know the truth. You have that right. I know that. I would never try to keep something like this from you. But I was so disoriented at first."

"Of course you were." I feel like I'm struggling to get my feet under me. I can't quite process what I'm being told. She's pregnant? And there's only one reason she would be breaking down like this telling me about it—it must be my baby. Of course, it is. I'm not aware of her having been with anyone else, which isn't to say she *couldn't* have been—but we've been spending so much time together lately that I can't imagine how that could have happened without my noticing.

It's *my* baby.

My God. I'm going to be a father?

It's the last news in the world I ever expected to hear. Becoming a parent was never a part of my plan.

"You don't have to do anything," Pamela says quickly. "I'm not asking you for anything, Christos. But I needed you to know. I can't have this baby without at least giving you the opportunity to be a part of its life. Whatever you want is okay, but you have a right to the information. And now that I've told you...I've done what I had to do."

She watches me, her eyes full of fear and hope.

Chapter 25
Pamela

Having told him the truth feels like coming up for air. It feels like I can breathe again for the first time since I learned I was pregnant. I know that whatever response he gives me, I will be all right.

If he's angry, if he throws me out of this hospital room and never wants to see me again, that will be okay. That will teach me something about the type of man he is, and God, I hope the father of my child isn't that type of man. But I'll be able to handle it.

What matters most to me right now is that he's alive. If he's alive and wants nothing more to do with me and our baby, that still isn't as bad as if he had died. I can handle anything else now that the worst possible outcome isn't the one that's happened. Anything else is fine.

At least, that's what I'm telling myself. That's what I need to believe to get me through these next few moments—the moments after I've told him and before he's answered when there's no going back and any response is possible.

"I can't believe you're being so honest with me," he says.

I don't understand. "Of course, I'm being honest," I say, even though it's a little disingenuous to say *of course* when I wasn't sure myself whether or not I was going to tell him when I went back and forth on it dozens of times before making my final decision. "You have a right to know. This affects you too. You're going to be a parent as much as I am. I couldn't have kept it from you."

"But I haven't earned your honesty," he says quietly.

"What do you mean?"

"The land. I know things between us fell apart because I didn't tell you I made an offer on the same property your father did," he says. "I know the problem wasn't only that I wanted to buy that land. The problem was that I didn't tell you when I knew that the two of us were competing over it."

Now that he says it out loud, I know he's right—that's exactly the problem. "I wish you had told me," I admit.

"I know," he agrees. "I should have told you. I should have come to you when I knew we were both trying to buy the same property. Maybe we could have come to an arrangement. We could have negotiated something. I don't know. It's a pretty big plot of land. Maybe we could have split it, or...*something*. I don't know what the solution would have been, but I know that keeping it to myself was wrong, and I'm sorry I did it."

"Don't worry about that now," I tell him. I grab the chair in the room and pull it close to his bed so I can sit down beside him. "That doesn't matter anymore."

"Of course it matters," he says. "It does matter, Pamela. I want you to know that *I* know it does. That land was important to you. I understand that now."

"It was important to you too," I say.

"It was. It is. But we could have had a conversation about it. We *should* have done that." He takes a breath. "We still should."

I wonder what that means. Is he saying he might consider not buying after all, that he might be willing to let Dad buy the land? I don't know—but I don't want to push it. Not today. The truth is that I don't care very much about that land anymore. I almost lost him. That fact is putting everything else into perspective. No dreams I had of creating new wine varietals and working with famous chefs are as important as the fact that I can sit here and have this conversation with Christos. At the very least, he won't die without knowing that he's going to be a father. That was what I feared most of all.

"The land doesn't matter so much right now," I say.

"Not as much as the baby," he agrees with a smile. "I'm so grateful that you told me, Pamela. I know you didn't have to do that."

"It was the right thing to do," I say.

"I'm glad you think so. I hope I can earn that."

"You don't have to earn anything. You don't have to do anything." I don't want him feeling beholden to me. I'm finding it hard to think of anything worse than that.

But he shakes his head. "I know I don't have to do anything," he says, reaching for my hand. "I want to, Pamela. I want to be with you. I always wanted that. I didn't want us to split up like we did, leaving things unfinished. I've hated being away from you. I know neither of us was planning on this, but I've been happier since I've known you than at any other point in my life, and I'm not about to give that up. And now, with this baby on the way—well, there's no question about what I want to do here—if you'll have me, that is."

"If I'll have you?" I hear what he's saying, but I'm afraid to believe it.

"I want to be with you," he says again. "Will you take me back? Whatever has to happen with the land—"

"Nothing has to happen with the land," I say quickly. "I don't want it to be like that, or to feel I'm back with you conditionally. I want to be with you too, Christos. I want us to be a family. I want this baby to know its father and grow up with two parents, and I want us to pick up where we left off. The land—that can be between you and my father. I don't need to be involved. I don't *want* to be involved. I'll be happy either way if we raise this baby together. I don't need anything else."

Christos smiles and takes my hand. "I hoped you would say that," he says quietly. "It's all I want too, Pamela, I promise."

Tears are spilling freely down my cheeks now. I leave my chair and move carefully onto the bed beside Christos. He's holding out his arms, and I manage to squeeze in next to him and curl up with my head on his shoulder, without disturbing the bandages, IVs, or the many wires running from his body to the machines in the room. Christos wraps his arm around my shoulders and runs his fingers slowly up and down my arm.

I let my eyes slip shut. It's so good to be held by him again—I can't quite believe it's happening, after all the anxiety and fear I've been through, after all the devastation of our argument and the realization that he had gone into danger without even saying goodbye to me. I don't know how I'm going to live with the idea that he has this dangerous job that can take him away from me without warning at any time. And that'll be even more challenging to live with once there's a baby in the picture—knowing that at any moment, my child could be fatherless.

But it's not a good enough reason to keep me from him. I would rather my child have a father and lose him than never have one at all. Christos wants to be a part of our lives. For right now, that's good enough.

No, not *good enough*. It's *wonderful*. It's more than I dared to wish for on the plane ride here, fighting back tears and not knowing whether he was going to live or die, not knowing whether he'd want to see me at his side if he opened his eyes. It's more than I dreamed of during the long hours I spent sitting beside his bed and praying that he would wake up.

All I wanted, all I asked for, was that he would live. And not only is alive, but he wants a life with me. It's too much. I can't think about our land struggles. Not anymore. I don't care what happens there as long as I can be allowed to keep this.

"Are you okay?" Christos murmurs.

"I—" I can't find words to express my feelings. I am more than okay, but I'm also so utterly overwhelmed that a part of me wants to close my eyes and fall asleep right here.

He seems to understand. He leans over and presses a kiss on my forehead. "We can talk later," he says. "For now, let's be happy that we found each other again and will be together. And we're going to have a baby." He lets out a little chuckle. "I can't believe it. That's still sinking in. I'm going to be a father."

"Are you happy about it?"

"I couldn't be any happier," he assures me. "Shocked, yes, and there's plenty to think about, arrangements to make—but yes, I'm incredibly happy. I can't believe how lucky we are, that this is happening to us."

I move up on the bed so my mouth finds his for a passionate kiss, and it's enough to chase all my worries away.

Chapter 26
Christos

"You didn't have to do all this," I tell Pam as she helps me through the front door and into her little cottage. "It wasn't like I couldn't afford the hospital stay."

"Don't be silly. I wasn't going to leave you alone in that hospital miles from home," she says. "I want you at home with me."

"I don't want to be an inconvenience to you."

"Always thinking about someone other than yourself," she said.

I have to laugh. "I never thought I'd hear you describe me like that. I thought you thought I was one of the most selfish people you had ever met."

"Oh, I still think that," she says. "I don't know how to account for it, but I think both things are true about you."

I hiss in pain as I ease myself down onto the edge of the bed. "Well, I guess I had it in me to surprise you," I say. "That's nice to know."

"Let's get this off," Pamela suggests, her hands moving to the buttons of my shirt.

I chuckle. "We've been back for less than five minutes and you're already trying to get me naked? Aren't you tired from that drive?" We had to rent a car to get back because my doctors wouldn't approve me for a flight so soon after my surgery.

"I'm restless from that drive," she says. "I want to do something. If you think you're up for it, I mean."

"Hell, when it comes to you, I'm always up for it," I tell her.

"We'll be careful." She pushes me down onto my back gently. "You have to let me do all the work, okay?"

"I think I can handle that," I say.

She smiles at me and pulls off her shirt.

I'm instantly hard. God, the sight of her is enough to knock me out. I can't believe I almost lost this, and I can't believe I'm lucky enough to be getting it back when I have done nothing to make me worthy of her.

I know I'm supposed to let her do all the work, but I can't resist reaching up to take her breasts in my hands. They feel like they were made for me to hold. The size, the weight, the way her head falls back and she lets out a moan of ecstasy when my thumbs brush over her nipples even lightly...I want to fuck her, but I also want to stay here and do this for a while. I want to see how much I can work her up first.

There's nothing like a near-death experience to make you want to grab life by the throat.

I sit up, scoot back on the bed, and lean against the headboard. "Come here," I tell her.

It's a mark of the chemistry we share, she doesn't try to argue. She doesn't protest that I'm supposed to take it easy or that we agreed she'd take the lead here. She crawls into my open arms and settles between my legs, leaning back against my chest and letting me adjust her so that she isn't putting any pressure on my wound.

She *is* putting pressure on my cock, though, *holy shit*. I move a little behind her, grinding against her back, and she pushes back into me. I'm not going to pretend there isn't a part of me that aches to hump her like this until I come...God, she makes me feel like a damn teenager sometimes—but there is so much more I want right now, and I'm not about to lose sight of that.

I trace her nipples slowly with my fingertips and then rub the undersides as they harden up. She inhales sharply.

She's squirming in my arms and it's doing interesting things to the friction against my cock. If I'm not careful with this, we might both come, and that's not what I want. I want to fuck her. I need to be inside her. But I won't rob myself of this, watching her fall apart in my arms at the slightest touch. I think I can get her there.

I massage her breasts for a moment. She melts back into me, humming with pleasure, but also relaxing fully, which I know she needs to reach orgasm. Once all the tension has left her body, I work my fingers slowly toward her nipples again.

She starts to breathe faster, unevenly. *Fuck,* I'm hard. I wonder if I could come just *listening* to her.

I circle her nipples with my thumbs and bring her closer. She arches desperately into my touch, as I lick and suck her breasts. Her legs spread wide and her hips bucking. I know she wants more, but I'm not giving it to her yet. Not until—

"Oh—fuck, Chris, I—"

She's never called me that before. She only calls me by my full name. It feels insanely intimate to hear that nickname on her lips, even though *Chris* is what most people call me most of the time. I don't know how to explain it—coming from her, it's special.

She thrashes in my arms as she comes. "Yes, baby," I groan, sucking her nipples hard through it. "Come for me. That's it. You're so fucking hot, don't stop." God, she could sell tickets to this. She'd pack stadiums.

She rolls away from me, and I'm expecting her to go limp with exhaustion—it would be understandable if she did. But instead, she climbs on top of me and sinks onto my hard, throbbing cock, and it's only once I'm buried inside her that I fully realize how fucking much

I've needed her. I never want her to get off. I'm so glad she already came once because it means I can now set the pace and we can make this last as long as I want it to.

I want it to last a long damn time. "Slowly," I breathe.

"Am I hurting you?" Her eyes are full of concern.

"Not at all," I assure her. "I don't know when I've felt so good. I don't want it to end."

She smiles at me. "We have all night."

"All night sounds pretty fucking perfect to me," I tell her.

She starts to move on me, and I swear, it's like that bullet did kill me because this has got to be heaven. Every time she moves, she sends waves of ecstasy crashing through me. This is different from any sex we've had before. Her fingertips trace the lines of my scar, and her touch lingers, igniting a heat that drives my cock even larger. The way her eyes lock onto mine, full of desire and a hint of mischief, sends a surge of anticipation through me. Her hands drift lower, teasing and deliberate, pulling me closer until there's no space left between us.

I resist the urge to come. All I want is to be inside her, joined with her like this. All I want is to never be apart again.

I don't know when I turned into such a sap. Probably around the time she told me she was having my baby.

Our hands map each other's bodies like we're afraid we might forget, the slow, grinding rhythm of her body, the wet heat of her, our sweat mingling together. Her breath catches as I press my lips to her neck, tasting the salt on her skin, and she melts against me. My hands trace the curve of her waist, and down her front, slipping a finger into her, finding her clit, feeling the soft, smooth warmth of her. She arches into my touch, seeking more of the connection we share.

I'm out of my mind with arousal and desire a moment before it begins, my orgasm radiates through my body, and as I come inside her, the feeling is the same. She comes again as I do, clenching around me, her eyes closed and her body stretched out gloriously, delighting in sensations. When she finishes, she rolls to one side instead. I know she has to because of my injury, but I still hate it. I want no distance at all between our bodies. I pull her in close and she rests her head against my shoulder.

It's unlike any I've ever had before—not the usual sudden burst of ecstasy, but a slow and gradual build that transitions so seamlessly into the peak of my pleasure that I almost don't notice the difference.

I lose track of time, we've fuck for hours. It's the most erotic thing I've ever experienced in my life—

The sun is starting to rise behind her, making her skin glow. I've never seen anything so beautiful in all my life.

Neither of us says anything. It doesn't feel like there's anything that needs to be said.

We still have plenty of things to figure out. But right now, today, it's enough that we're together. Everything else can be solved as long as we're in each other's lives. And as I lie here with my arm around Pam, breathing in time with her, I know I'll never let anything come between us again.

Chapter 27
Pamela

"So now you're telling me you want us to go into business together?" Dad raises his eyebrows skeptically. "I find that difficult to believe, Chris."

"My cards are on the table here," Christos says. "I'll sign over the land for the expanded vineyard to you. My only condition is you let me join your team as a partner. You don't need to pay me, you can let me have a small portion of the profits. Twenty percent?"

"That's not right," I cut in. I knew he would lowball the situation, and I won't let him get away with it. "If you're giving us enough land to double our holdings, *and* you're going to work on the property with us, you should get fifty percent."

"No," Dad cuts in. "I'm willing to consider this proposition, but it's not going to be a fifty-fifty split."

"No, I agree, it shouldn't be," Christos said. "Pamela's kind to me. But you built this business from the ground up, Matt. You should retain the lion's share of the profits, and me buying into it doesn't change that fact."

"I think thirty percent seems fair," Dad says.

Christos smiles. "I'd certainly take that."

"But you can't disappear all the time," Dad lectures. "That type of thing was fine when you were a volunteer, but if you're going to be a partner, I need to be able to find you at all times. We can't have these situations where you go missing for weeks. I can't work with that."

"That's not going to be an issue," Christos assures Dad.

Dad raises his eyebrows. "It isn't?"

"I won't be taking off like that anymore."

"Can I count on that? You say it now, but I don't want to revisit this issue in three months and to hear you say you *thought* things would change but something came up..."

"No, I can vouch for Christos here," I added. "He means what he says."

"I was working a second job," Christos explains. "When I was away, it was because of the demands of that job. But it no longer makes sense to split my time that way. Now that Pam and I are starting a family, I'll be here and available full-time. I've changed my role with my company to make this possible."

Nothing could have made me happier than I was the day he came home and told me he'd sold a part of his company to his partner and stepped away from active missions with his ex-Navy SEALs. I know that work meant a lot to him, and I wondered if he might regret giving it up, but he's perfectly happy since then, and he reassured me that his SEAL teams could manage without him. "It's the one good thing to come out of my injury," he explained. "I saw how they would function without me, and they did an amazing job. Different teams will continue to thrive in my absence, and people will still be saved."

"It is good," I told him. "I need you now. This baby needs you."

"And this is exactly where I want to be," he assured me. "Besides, it's not as if I won't be part of the company anymore. I'll still be the point person with the government. I'll stay on the strategy side to help plan missions and I'll continue to develop future tech. That's always been my true passion. I won't go into the field anymore—I'll be able to stay with the family."

We were in bed together when that conversation happened. We've been spending a lot of time in bed over the past couple of weeks—it feels like we're making up for lost time. Regardless, that isn't something I'll tell my father, or anyone for that matter. Dad has accepted my pregnancy—I think he's even excited for me, although he isn't about to admit it out loud. But accepting my relationship with Christos is another thing altogether. I think it still bugs Dad that his friend, who's only a little younger than him, is involved with his daughter. He'll get used to it, and we can be patient until he does.

The upshot is that I can't explain to Dad what makes me feel so confident that Christos isn't splitting his focus anymore. I know he won't, but Dad will have to take him at his word about it.

"As long as you're planning on sticking around," Dad says, "I think we'll be able to do business."

"Hey, the first time I go AWOL, you can write me out of the ownership of the vineyard. Put it in the contracts."

Dad looks skeptical, but he offers a slow nod. "I know how important this is to Pam," he says, "That's why I'm doing it. You understand? She's had her heart set on this land and on the opportunities it will open up for MacLaine's."

I know both Dad and Brian really like Christos. How could they not? He is built like a barge, a hard worker, a fast learner, and handsome as anybody has the right to be.

"That's why I'm doing it too," Christos says. "I don't want you to ever doubt my feelings for your daughter, Matt. I care about her a great deal. We've been through some hard times, but I would do anything to make her happy. I'd hand over that parcel of land and walk away if she asked me to."

"You know I don't want that," I tell him quickly.

He smiles at me. "I know you don't," he says. "I'm glad you don't. I'd walk away from you if you asked me to, but I think it might kill me to do it."

"All right, all right," Dad interjects. "That's enough of that. You two can sweet talk to each other when you're on your own, but for the love of God, don't do it in front of me. I don't need to hear all that."

Christos nods. I know he thinks the best thing to do is to comply with anything Dad asks. I won't argue about it, but I don't agree. I think Dad needs to get used to the idea that the two of us will be around each other, that we're in love with each other and aren't going to hide it. If Dad wants to call it sweet talking, that's okay with me, but it's a lot deeper than that, and a lot more important. Our feelings aren't going away, so Dad has to get comfortable with them. It's the only option he has.

"I suppose she's told you about her ambitions," Dad says to Christos.

"She has," Christos says. "And I couldn't be more excited. Of course, I don't know as much as you do about wine, and I certainly don't know as much as you about crafting new varietals, but I'm eager to see what Pam will come up with. And we've already had some discussions about chefs we might want to try to hire for the restaurant when it's open, although, of course, we'd defer to you when it comes to that."

He's being a little over the top about it. We don't have to defer to Dad on every decision. But it's working because Dad seems to appreciate what Christos is saying. He smiles and nods. "That sounds perfect," he says. "We'll have a longer conversation about this later—we need to decide what cuisine we'll serve as well."

"I have thoughts about that." Because my education was in France, my dream is to work in a French restaurant. I know the most about French wines and how to pair different varietals with French foods, so it will be the best choice if we want to be successful. I'm sure both Dad and Christos will let me have my way when it comes to this—it's hard to imagine either of them arguing when they know the restaurant is my dream and vision.

"I think our first step is to have your name added to the land deed," Christos says to Dad. "And I've taken the liberty of preparing the documents, so if you agree, we can sign the paperwork right now if you feel ready."

I can tell Dad wasn't ready for that. He glances at me as if to see what to say, but I don't have anything to contribute. Whatever he does right now, it has to be his decision alone. I don't want to hear him tell me later that I badgered him into something he wasn't sure he wanted. Until he signs those documents of his own free will, I'm not saying another word.

Dad and Christos move to the table. Christos brings out the papers and sets them down in front of Dad, and he begins to read them. My heart is pounding in my chest. I can't believe this is happening. After everything we've been through, all the time I spent thinking it wasn't going to happen, now, at last, the land will be ours together. I'll build what I've dreamed—and one thing I never thought would come of this is Christos. Our baby. Our family.

I spent so much time thinking about what I had lost when I found out Christos was buying that land. I never anticipated that this would end with me getting more than I dared to wish for. And yet, as Dad picks up his pen and begins to sign, I know that that's exactly what's happening.

Everything I dreamed of, and more, is coming true.

Chapter 28
Pamela

We make it home from Dad's house, I feel like a powder keg about to explode. The door is barely closed behind us when we start taking off our clothes.

I'm fully expecting Christos to make some crack about my lack of self-control, but when I turn to face him he's halfway out of his pants himself. I feel like dropping to my knees and taking him in my mouth right then and there. All I want is to be closer to him.

But this isn't going to be like the last few times we've been together. He's healed from his injury now, so we don't have to be as careful with one another as we have been. It means he can finally have his way with me, the way I know he's been wanting to since we got back together.

I can't pretend I haven't been quietly looking forward to this moment, but it was one of those things I didn't dare talk about because I didn't want to put pressure on him to rush into acting like he had recovered before he had.

He is now. I can tell. It's so obvious from the color in his cheeks and the way he's looking at me like he wants to devour me.

He advances on me in two short strides, and even though I trust Christos Tzavaras with my life, there's a second when I'm genuinely a little fearful. He is so big, so strong, he could do anything he wanted to do with me right now. Since I don't know what he has planned this is intimidating and thrilling.

He picks me up and tosses me over his shoulder as lightly as if I were a sack of cotton balls. I let out a squeal that I wouldn't have thought myself capable of—but Christos has brought all kinds of new things out in me, and I'm not ashamed to admit that.

He carries me to the bedroom and places me gently on the bed. Standing at the foot of it and surveying me with a hungry look in his eyes, he allows a slow smile to spread over his face. "You look delicious," he murmurs. "You're the most gorgeous thing I've ever seen."

I'm finding it hard to breathe, looking up at him, watching him strip off his pants so that he's naked. In a moment he's going to be on top of me, inside of me, as I watch his cock rise slowly, I want it so bad it hurts. I feel my hips lift toward him, off the bed, of their own accord, as if I'm being magnetically drawn to him somehow.

He chuckles low in his throat. "I fucking love watching you when you're all turned on like this," he murmurs. "Maybe I'll do this for a while. That could be fun. See how crazed you get before I finally touch you. What do you think?"

"Don't you fucking dare," I groan. "Do you know how hard it was for me to keep my hands off you when we were at my father's house?"

"Mmm, you didn't keep your hands off me, though." He kneels between my legs, and I swear it's like his cock is reaching out for me. I almost don't even have to look—the tension between us is so potent that I can feel his desire for me like it's a physical presence. "Your hands were all over me. That's why your dad was so pissed off. You kept touching me."

"You were doing that too," I point out.

"Yeah. I think he liked that even less."

"But that's not what I mean. I could have pulled you into a closet and fucked you there, with my father in the next room. I *wanted* to do that. I still do. It's probably going to happen at some point."

He grins wolfishly. "You want to fuck me at your dad's house?"

"I want to fuck you *everywhere*, Christos, are you—*oh*—"

His hand is between my legs, toying with me, and I can't remember what the hell point I was about to make. I lift my hips to him, feeling wanton and desperate, grinding against his hand.

He chuckles. "Some other time," he promises, withdrawing his hand. "That's not what I want to do today."

"You are such a fucking *tease*, I swear to God…"

"Don't worry, honey, I got you." He covers my body with his, his cock settling between my legs, and it is such a small fraction of what I want from him, but it's still better than nothing. I wrap my legs around him and pull him as close as I can get him. I can feel him throbbing against me in time with his breathing, and it is utterly exquisite.

His hips jerk, and I feel a surge of satisfaction—he's starting to lose control now. He's not going to be able to keep this up much longer. All I have to do is wait him out, and then I'll get what I need so badly.

"You're being so patient," he murmurs, rocking against me. "I'm gonna give it to you so good."

"Now?"

He chuckles. "I love you when you want it this bad, you know. It makes me want to make you wait for it."

"You don't want to make me wait for it." I hook my legs behind his back and tilt my hips a bit so he slides into me—not much, but enough to make him groan and give in altogether.

He grips my shoulders and slams into me as hard as he can. It hurts so good, and it's wonderful.

I wrap all my limbs around him as if I can somehow drive him deeper into me than he already is. I want to absorb his body into mine. We're moving in such an easy, natural rhythm that I don't even have to think about it, and I'm losing track of where one of us ends and the other begins. It's like we're fully united, one body moving together.

I feel him start to come before it happens. It begins in his abdomen, which becomes tense and hard, and I don't have to question it because I understand on a visceral level what's happening. And without thought, his high pushes me toward my own, and I feel myself reach the edge and fall over it. I'm screaming his name, and my body rises to meet his, and it has all been worth the wait. I would go through every bit of what the two of us have dealt with so far all over again if it meant reaching this point, falling apart with pleasure while he thrust into me.

I'm shaking when he finishes. He goes limp on top of me and doesn't bother to roll away, and I don't want him to. It feels so perfect having him here. I wrap my arms around him and press my lips gently to his shoulder in a soft kiss.

"I want to marry you," he murmurs.

"What?" I must be mishearing him.

He pushes himself up on his forearms to look me in the eye. "I've never loved anyone like I love you," he says. "We're going to have a family together. I don't know what we're waiting for anymore. I want us to live in the same house, to fall asleep with you every night and wake up with you every morning. I want this to be our life, and I'm ready for us to start living it. Will you marry me?"

"I—" I sit up in bed to face him properly. I never expected anything like this. I know we're back together. We're having this baby. But even so, Christos has never seemed like the marrying kind. I wasn't even sure I was the marrying kind.

But everything he's offering me now sounds beyond ideal, and I want every bit of it.

"Hang on," he says suddenly, getting out of bed. He leaves the room. I frown. What is this about?

He's back with something in his hand—I can't see what it is. He drops to one knee by the side of the bed, and everything falls into place.

It's a ring.

This is a real proposal.

He's not asking me if I'd like to get married abstractly. He is honest to God asking me to marry him.

He holds up the ring, and it's beautiful—a round brilliant-cut diamond solitaire. But all I can focus on is his face. The face of the man I love, who is asking me if he can love me for the rest of our lives.

"Marry me," he whispers.

And there's only one possible answer in my mind.

"Yes," I whisper. "I will marry you."

The moment he slips the ring onto my finger feels somehow impossible and inevitable at the same time. He gets to his feet, pulls me up with him, wraps his arms around me, and presses my lips in a kiss.

It's the best thing I've ever felt. It's the happiest moment of my life so far.

And the truly amazing thing is that, even as he kisses me and I feel the weight of the ring on my finger, I know that this is only the beginning.

There are so many beautiful moments yet to come.

Chapter 29
Christos

Six Months Later

"I'm surprised the two of you wanted to combine your wedding with the restaurant opening," Brian admits. The two of us are lingering outside the restaurant and smoking a couple of cigars,—he said there was too much to celebrate to let the moment pass us by, I agree. It feels extremely fraternal to be standing here doing this with him, and I've never had a brother before. The idea of sharing something like this with someone is an exciting one.

"The restaurant means everything to Pamela," I explain. "I think she's as excited about this as she is about the baby."

"I don't know about that," Brian says, laughing. "I've never seen my sister as excited about anything as she is about the baby."

"Well, fair enough," I say with a smile. Watching Pamela anticipate becoming a mother has been a truly wonderful experience, and I think Brian is right—it means more to her than anything else that's going on in our lives. "But it has her more excited than the wedding does." Not the marriage, maybe, but the wedding itself. I know Pamela is excited about today's festivities, and so am I, but she's not the sort to romanticize her wedding day. When I asked her if she wanted to put it off until after the baby was born, thinking that her pregnancy might prevent her from being able to pick out her dream gown or something, she laughed and told me there was no reason to do that. "I want to be married to you," she explained. "I'd marry you today in jean shorts and a bikini top. I don't care what we wear."

That outfit was tempting. If she'd wanted to do it, I would. Instead, she's wearing a white cotton sundress that flatters her growing belly, and she's never looked more beautiful to me. I'm glad we didn't wait until after the baby was born. There's something so special about seeing the woman I love carrying my child, and I wouldn't have wanted to miss out on the opportunity to marry her like this. Rose Crawford has been walking around with a camera snapping photos all day, and I know those pictures will be meaningful to me.

We finish our cigars and change into fresh jackets so that we won't bring the aroma of them around Pamela—this was her condition for allowing us to go out for a smoke, and I thought it was reasonable.

The inside of the restaurant is full of people who live in town, all of whom came out to enjoy the wedding ceremony and the first service here at the restaurant following that. Amazingly, so many people wanted to be here for this—I know most of them—Pamela and her family have assured me that this is what to expect around here. Everyone knows one another. Everyone has friendships that span decades. These people watched Pamela grow up. They aren't about to miss out on her wedding day. There's something pretty special about that.

I find her behind the bar. "You shouldn't be working today," I tell her, leaning across the counter to kiss her. "This is our wedding day. You should leave this stuff to someone else."

"It's just to get things started," Pam counters with a smile. "And today is opening day. I'll leave it in the hands of my team in a minute. Besides, I'm having a good time, Christos. This is exactly where I want to be."

"Can I at least come back there and help you?" I ask her. "You're my wife. We ought to be a team."

"I'd love that," she says. "But you have to do everything I tell you to do."

"Yes, ma'am." That's extremely hot. I walk behind the counter, take the apron she hands me, and tie it around my waist. "Tell me what to do."

"Get a couple of bottles of the Merlot. We need to pour some glasses for everyone who had the lamb."

I get the wine out and start filling glasses, and because I ordered the lamb myself, I hang onto one of them. someone will refill it before the dinner course is served, but that's all right. I'm excited about this meal—the chef we've hired to run the restaurant has cooked for Pamela and me a few times, and he's amazing. I know Pamela is thrilled to be working with him too. It feels like things couldn't be working out any better for the two of us.

Rose approaches the counter, camera in hand. "All right, lovebirds," she says, holding it up. "Give us a smile."

I put my arm around Pamela. She leans into me and relaxes, and without even looking at her, I can imagine the smile on her face.

"I need a word with the two of you if you have a moment," Rose says.

"Sure," I agree. I wipe my hands on my apron. "We're finished here, right, Pamela?"

"Anything for you, Rose." She puts down the bottle and steps around the bar. "Is everything all right?"

"Everything is fine," Rose assures us. "More than fine,—I'm so happy for the two of you. I know you both had your eye on my little cottage over the past year."

My breath catches. Is she finally ready to consider selling the house? The timing couldn't be any better. Pamela and I have been living there since we got engaged, but we've known the whole time that it might not last. Though we have my big house next door to move into when the time comes, we've admitted to ourselves and each other that it wouldn't be our first choice. We love the cottage so much that we both want to stay there if the opportunity presents itself. But until now, it's always seemed to us like Rose would never be willing to sell. It has felt like a losing battle.

"You know I haven't wanted to sell that place," Rose says. "But I've never told either of you why that is."

"I thought you were too attached to it to want to sell," Pam says.

"I am," Rose agrees. "I'm attached to the memories I have of that place. I raised my children there, and it meant the world to me. And I always thought that if the house ever went to someone else, I would want it to be a family. I'd want to think of new parents raising their children there."

I'm speechless. It sounds like she *is* ready to talk about selling. But I don't want to get my hopes up too high, because I know Pamela and I both want this so badly and it seems too good to be true.

"I couldn't tell you that," Rose continues. "I didn't want you to feel judged in any way, or pressured into a lifestyle that wasn't right for you. Not everyone wants to become a parent, and I've always been so fond of you both. It never mattered to me what you chose for yourselves. I couldn't picture the house without a family in it, though, and now...well, now it seems like that could happen."

"Are you saying you're willing to sell to us?" Pamela asks breathlessly.

"Not exactly," Rose says. "I've made you both wait too long for this, and I feel terrible about it. I want to do something to make it up to you and show you how much I care about you and support your union. I want to give you the cottage as a wedding gift."

Pamela gasps.

I shake my head. "Rose—you can't give us a gift like that. It's too much. We want the cabin, but please let us pay you for it."

"I wouldn't hear of it," Rose says firmly. "I don't need the money, and it does need a little fixing up. I'm not going to use the cottage anymore. The only thing that mattered to me was seeing it in the hands of someone who could get everything I did out of it, and now I know that's the two of you. And because you're married, I don't have to choose which one of you should have it. This couldn't have worked out any more neatly."

"Are you sure about this?" Pamela asks. "You know how much I love that cottage, and I'm so grateful to you for the offer, but that's such a big gift. I can't possibly accept unless I know you're sure."

"All I ask in return is that you let me come over and visit with you and that baby sometimes," Rose says with a smile.

Pamela smiles back. "Well, that we can do, and I'm sure it will be often," she says. "Thank you so much, Rose. You have no idea what this means to us."

"I think I do," Rose says. "And that's why I know you're the right people to live in the house that always meant so much to me. No one else could appreciate the place the way the two of you would, and I wouldn't entrust it to any other family."

Pamela hugs her, and then I find myself doing the same. It seems as if all our dreams are coming true. I don't know how the two of us could be so lucky, I have never felt happier or more blessed in all my life.

Chapter 30
Pamela

One Year Later

"Devon's only recently started sitting up," I tell Rose. The two of us are sitting on the beach with my son between us. Devon's picking up handfuls of sand, methodically adding them to a pile in front of him.

"He sure is good at it," Rose says, beaming at him. "What a big strong boy you're raising! You must be so proud of him."

"We are very happy," I say. "Of course, all that matters to us is that he's happy and healthy—but it is exciting to watch him learn new things. I can't wait until he's old enough to say his first words. You know, Christos is trying to rig the game by teaching him words ahead of time."

"Is he?"

"Every night, he sings what he calls "The Daddy Song," I say, laughing. "The only words are "Daddy, Daddy, Daddy," and he holds Devon in his arms and dances around the room while he does it. He says he's trying to create a positive association with the word so that Devon will start asking for it."

"And after all that, I'd be willing to bet you anything his first word will be 'Mama'," Rose says. "You can't control these things! I was so excited to hear my eldest's first word."

"And what was it?"

She shakes her head. "*Socks.*"

"Seriously?"

"I don't know. He liked socks a lot. He still does, as it turns out. Asks for them every Christmas."

I laugh. "It must be rewarding to see them grow from baby to adulthood."

"You're in for the journey of a lifetime," Rose agrees. "It'll be the best thing that ever happened to you. I'm so glad I get to watch you have this experience. I know it would have meant the world to your mother, too."

"Having you here for this almost makes it feel like she's with me because the two of you were such good friends," I tell Rose. "If I can't have her here, you're the next best thing."

Rose wraps an arm around my shoulders. "Are we going to open that bottle?" she asks me.

"It's not perfect," I tell her. "It will take a few more seasons to get it how I want it. That's why I haven't put the label on it yet." The label for the new varietal is a single red rose. I didn't print any words on it, because the image speaks for itself. My new Riesling Blush is exactly what I dreamed of producing, and I named it after the woman who gave me my home. It's the icing on the cake.

"I'd still like to try it," Rose says enthusiastically. "Every phase of this process is interesting to me. I know it isn't finished, but I can't wait to see what you've got so far."

I pull out the bottle and the corkscrew and start to uncork it.

"Ah!" Rose said. "And here's that handsome husband of yours."

I look up. Sure enough, Christos is walking down the path. "How are things at the vineyard?" I ask him as he sits beside us and hands me the extra glass he brought from the house.

"About the same as always," he says. "Nonstop work. Your father sure is driving the students hard this season."

"I think it's a great idea to host student volunteers," Rose says. "Having them around will help you get the work done, and it'll let them figure out if they're interested in taking on full-time work at the vineyard after they graduate. It's a good way to let people experience the work as they get college credit before making a bigger commitment. You will find yourselves with many new loyal employees this way."

"And it also gives people a chance to learn more about wine," I add. "That's the part I like best—the classes we teach after hours." Most people who volunteer at the vineyard now do so because they are interested in wine and want to learn more. I open classes to the public at intervals and get a great turnout, but I offer them to our volunteers so they earn credit, and I know they enjoy them. It's been one of the best parts of our newly expanded business.

I finish uncorking the wine, pour some into a glass, and hand it to Rose. "You can go ahead and try it," I say, reaching for Christos' glass next. "Don't wait on us."

She takes a sip. "This is wonderful," she says. "I expected it to taste like that blend you served me in your kitchen last year. Don't get me wrong—that was also good. But this is much better!"

"It isn't finished yet," I say again. "There's more work to do to get the grapes where I want them—there was no way I could get it right in one season. But I think I'm on the right track."

"You are," Rose agrees. "I can't wait to see this on shelves. Every time I see it in a store, I'll have to let all my friends it's special because it's named after me!"

"We'll make sure you get as much as you could ever want free of charge, Rose," Christos says. "We wouldn't have been able to put as much work as we have into the vineyard if you weren't often here looking after Devon for us."

Devon reaches out his arms to Rose.

We all laugh. "Looks like he wants his grandma," Christos says. Even though Rose isn't family by blood, we've all taken to referring to her as Devon's grandmother and the two of them have embraced the relationship. I love watching them together. They love each other and seem so happy every time they are together.

Rose picks Devon up and cuddles him. "You are the sweetest little guy," she says. "I love that you're growing up in the house where I raised my children."

Devon gurgles at her.

"Can I take him down to the water?" she asks me.

"I don't see why not." Devon loves the water, and I trust Rose with everything I have.

She gets up and walks down the beach with him in her arms, leaving me alone with Christos. I rest my head on his shoulder and he gently kisses my forehead.

"What do you think about having another baby someday?" he asks me.

"I think that sounds amazing." I love being a mother, and it will be fun to see Devon with a little brother or sister. "Not too soon, though. Maybe when he's two."

"That sounds right to me," Christos agrees. "Maybe three or five altogether?"

I have to laugh at that. "We'll see how we feel after the second one," I tell him. "I'm not making any promises right now."

"Fair enough. I never thought I wanted a big family, but now that I see him, it's hard to imagine anything else. I can't wait to watch him grow up, but at the same time, I'm already missing the newborn stage."

"You want to have another baby so we can have a newborn again?" I tease him.

"Is that so wrong?"

"No. I'd like to have a newborn again myself. I even miss being pregnant, to tell you the truth. I would never have expected that, but it's such a magical time."

"Even though you can't drink wine while you're pregnant?" His shoulders shake with laughter.

"I think I can survive a few months without it," I say. Wine is my passion and always will be, but I love my family even more.

"I think so too," Christos agrees. He has a right to say it—for the bulk of my pregnancy, as a show of solidarity, he didn't do anything I couldn't do. No wine, no seafood, not even deli meats. He took a break from that on our wedding day, but for the rest of the time, he was right by my side. He's always been a dream come true when it comes to supporting me.

And I know I can count on his support for anything I need. That's how I know I'm ready to consider having another child with him. Whatever life throws our way, we will handle it the way we always have—together.

I turn around in his arms so that I can kiss him. The sounds and the smell of the surf of Good Harbor Bay are all around us, and I can hear Devon laughing merrily in the distance. It's hard to imagine anything better than the life I have. As I relax into Christos' touch, I know I wouldn't change it for anything in the world.

The End

Did you like this book?

If so, you are going to love Babby Daddy SEAL, check the next page for a sneak peek.

Or jump here directly to KDP and grab a copy. https://www.amazon.com/dp/B0BY79F9YV

SNEAK PEEK

BABY DADDY SEAL

AN AGE GAP, ENEMIES TO LOVERS ROMANCE

"Brian Grant?"

I swallowed the shot I was contemplating before turning to face the young woman who had approached me. She was dressed for a good time in a short leather skirt that showed off miles of tanned, muscular thighs and a crop top that made me want to touch her bare midriff.

She had my complete attention. I hadn't even planned on coming to the bar to hook up, but here we are.

"You've heard of me?" It wouldn't be the first time that had happened. Navy SEALs tend to attract groupies, probably because there are so few of us and because we're the best of the best.

And fuck it, I might have been in my late forties, but I wasn't out to pasture. If this hot young thing was looking for some fun, I would be happy to give it to her.

She leaned closer to me, her fingertips brushing my arm, and I thought, *I'm in*.

And then she grinned and said, "Of course, we know each other. You don't recognize me?"

Oh, fuck. I hadn't slept with her before, had I? I wracked my brains—but no, I was sure I would remember.

She laughed. "It's me," she said. "Alison Barrett." Henry's daughter."

"Alison Barrett? What are you doing in a bar? Are you twenty-one yet?"

Alison stood up straight and retorted, "I'm twenty-six."

"You're twenty-six?" My jaw dropped.

"It's been a while."

"You can say that again." Alison Barrett was a kid. She wasn't *hot*. Except, suddenly, she was. I couldn't keep my eyes from wandering to things I had never noticed about her before—the curve of her breasts, for one thing. And that ass—I'd always been an ass guy, but if Henry Barrett knew I was thinking about putting my hands up his daughter's skirt, he would beat the hell out of me.

"Can I buy you a drink?" I asked, even though I absolutely knew I should not buy Alison Barrett a drink.

But what was the harm? She was of age. And it was just a drink. It would be good to catch up with the kid.

She sat down beside me. "I was hoping you would!"

"You were, huh?" She was definitely flirting with me.

"I haven't talked to you in ages," she groaned. "Not since Dad retired from the SEALs."

I didn't want to sit at the bar with the newly hot Alison and talk about her father. "Tell me what's been going on with you."

"Not much." She moved close so that her knees were touching mine. "I finished my Masters of Finance and moved back here in June. Got a job." She hesitated. "I'm thrilled I ran into you."

"Yeah?"

"Promise not to laugh, but I always had a thing for you when I was younger." She rolled her eyes. "I'm sure you think that's silly."

I didn't. I'd known that actually—but what had been a harmless one-sided crush when Alison was a teenager suddenly seemed like it might have legs. There was nothing to stop me now except for the persistent sense that I probably shouldn't put my hands on her.

Then again, what Henry didn't know wasn't going to hurt him. And I could keep this at an appropriate level—a little harmless flirting in a bar. I mean, she *was* of age. And she was so hot that my pants were starting to feel uncomfortable.

You cannot fuck Henry Barrett's daughter. If he ever found out you did, he would murder you.

But would he murder me for sitting here with her like this? For slotting my thigh between hers so we could be closer together?

"Tell me about your job," I suggested.

I wasn't fooling anybody, not even myself. Getting her talking about something mundane was just an excuse to lean in closer to her so I could hear her over the bar's noise. I was sure Alison could see right through it. But it didn't seem to bother her in the slightest.

She leaned closer to me, too—so close that I could feel the warmth of her body and the heat of her breath when she spoke, and yeah, I was going to need to stop drinking right now and probably take a nice long shower when I got home. *Holy shit.*

"Oh, my job's boring," Alison chuckled. "Government work. Pushing papers around."

"Yeah?"

"Dad is happy. You know he's always wanted to see me in the public sector."

"I didn't know that." And we were talking about Henry again. Ethical considerations aside, it was impossible to enjoy my fantasies about pulling her into the bathroom and shoving that skirt she was wearing above her hips. At the same time, she begged me to fuck her senseless while also trying to think of her as my best friend's daughter. The two ideas did not go together.

"Tell me about *you*," Alison suggested.

"Me?"

"Are you still with the SEALs?"

"I am, yeah." Henry's early retirement was a move I respected for him but could never have chosen for myself. Being a part of the SEALs was who I was.

"How's that been going?"

"Pretty good. What about that drink I was going to buy you?"

She grinned. "Scotch on the rocks?"

I had to admit; that I'd expected her to ask for a screwdriver or something like that. Something youthful and girly. Maybe she was trying to impress me. Perhaps she didn't want me thinking of her as a kid.

Maybe she *wasn't* a kid.

Twenty-six was young, but not too young. I would have been putting the moves on Alison if she hadn't been Henry's daughter.

I flagged down the bartender. "Scotch on the rocks, and another one of these." I pushed the shot glass in his direction.

"Oh, are we doing shots?" Alison asked.

"I am. You don't need to be."

She rolled her eyes. "What are you drinking?"

"Whiskey."

"Okay, forget the scotch," she said to the bartender. "Bring me a shot of whiskey as well, please."

"You don't have to do that."

"Of course, I don't *have to do it*," she chuckled. "I'm not pledging a sorority. But it's fun to do shots with people, don't you think?"

"You can't have been doing shots for more than five minutes."

"I have been doing shots for years now."

I raised an eyebrow at her. "Underage drinking?"

"Dad told me stories about the two of you in BUD/S training," she dismissed. "And I know you weren't twenty-one when you did your training because Dad wasn't twenty-one when he did his training, and he's two years older than you."

"You know a lot."

"I've told you," She said placidly, "I've had a crush on you for ages."

"Do you have a crush on me now?"

What the hell was I doing, asking her that? It wasn't as if I could act on it if she did.

But I had to know. I was so fucking attracted to her. Maybe I was just trying to feed my fantasies—there was no doubt that it would be more fun to think about her later if I knew that she was also thinking about me.

And the chemistry between us was like nothing I'd felt in a very long time. It was surprising that the other people in the bar weren't picking up on it somehow and couldn't see the desire crackling around us.

It was surprising to me that I still hadn't touched her.

She leaned toward me and bit her lip.

Fuuuuck. She shouldn't have done that. Watching the way her lip gave just a little beneath the pressure of her teeth made me want to bite it myself.

I shifted in my seat. I was hard as hell. It felt like my cock was reaching for her. I wanted to grab her by the waist and lift her onto my lap from the barstool she was seated on. I wanted to push and pull on her hips, grind her against me.

Based on her demeanor, I wanted to see if she was as hot and wet as I assumed. I wanted to fuck her.

"Your shots," the bartender chirped in, interrupting the filthy fantasy playing out in my head.

I wanted to thank him, and I also wanted to punch him in the face.

Fuck, I was out of control here.

Alison grinned at me like she knew what was happening in my head. She picked up one of the shot glasses. "What are we drinking to?" she asked, her eyes lighting up.

Fucking pull yourself together, Brian.

Only years of military discipline enabled me to tear myself out of the fantasy and focus on the young woman in front of me and the reality of our situation. "To your father," I suggested.

As much as I hadn't wanted to think about her father, I thought it was probably necessary to do so. It was good for me. I needed to remember that this was Henry's daughter because I could not let myself forget that fact.

I wasn't willing to risk damaging a relationship with my oldest and best friend over this, no matter how badly I wanted her.

Alison grinned. "All right," she raised the glass. "To Dad."

We slammed back our shots. Alison's didn't go down as quickly as mine did, which I thought was to be expected. She didn't have as many years of experience as I did, no matter what age she'd started drinking. She coughed a little, and I signaled to the bartender, who nodded and appeared a moment later with a glass of seltzer water.

Alison looked at it and shook her head. "I don't need that."

"Don't show off. It's just a chaser. Drink it."

I expected her to make a fuss and refuse, but she shrugged and took a long drink. Then she set the glass down. "Another," she announced.

"What are we doing here, Alison?"

I was surprised I'd asked her so bluntly. I had no idea what answer I was looking for.

"Shots," Alison quipped.

Okay, that was fair enough. It was an answer to my question, after all. And I decided to take it at face value. I had asked her what this was meant to be. She was telling me that we were just drinking together and nothing more.

I could respect that.

It didn't matter that she was Henry's daughter. It didn't matter that I was nearly twice her age.

What mattered was that she had told me she wanted to drink with me and catch up on the past. She didn't want to take this any farther than that.

That was fair enough.

You'll have to read the rest of this steamy story on Amazon

https://www.amazon.com/dp/B0BY79F9YV

Have you read any of my other books? If not, Go HERE! to my Amazon Author page

https://www.amazon.com/stores/author/B0BY7HFLY4

Or search for Dakota Nash.

And stick with me for more steamy romance!

Made in United States
Troutdale, OR
05/29/2024